FUTURE ATTACK

FUTURE ATTACK

PROTECT THE PAST: DEFEND THE PRESENT & PRESERVE THE FUTURE IN THE NAME OF GLOBAL AND NATIONAL SECURITY INTEREST.

STEPHEN MICHAEL

FUTURE ATTACK
PROTECT THE PAST: DEFEND THE PRESENT
& PRESERVE THE FUTURE IN THE NAME OF
GLOBAL AND NATIONAL SECURITY INTEREST.

iUniverse books may be ordered through booksellers or by contacting:

iUniverse
1663 Liberty Drive
Bloomington, IN 47403
www.iuniverse.com
1-800-Authors (1-800-288-4677)

Because of the dynamic nature of the Internet, any web addresses or links contained in this book may have changed since publication and may no longer be valid. The views expressed in this work are solely those of the author and do not necessarily reflect the views of the publisher, and the publisher hereby disclaims any responsibility for them.

Any people depicted in stock imagery provided by Getty Images are models, and such images are being used for illustrative purposes only. Certain stock imagery © Getty Images.

ISBN: 978-1-5320-4875-3 (sc)
ISBN: 978-1-5320-4876-0 (e)

Library of Congress Control Number: 2018905450

Print information available on the last page.

iUniverse rev. date: 05/03/2018

CONTENTS

Special Thanks

I want to thank my wife, Bonnie, for being my better half and putting up with me.

Honorable mention goes out to Tom Blancey, a.k.a. Stephen Stamps.

In addition, a big shout-out goes to Seneca Valley High class of 1980.

Finally, I want to thank everyone who enjoys reading my novels.

Προτεχτ τηε παστ, σεχυρε τηε πρεσεντ ανδ πρεσερϖε τηε φυτυρε. Τηισ ισ τηε μισσιον οφ τηε ΤΤΣΓ, Τιμε Τραϖελ Σεχτιον Γρουπ.[1]

[1] Protect the past, preserve the present, and defend the future.

ix

SECRET WARRIORS

Young Ronnie Slay doesn't notice the gold-framed photograph of President Ronald Reagan hanging on the wall. His eyes are glued to the television screen, which is broadcasting an army recruiting video of Army Commandos carrying huge backpacks wearing snug patrol caps.

Suddenly the video switches to Army Rangers standing in an aircraft, oxygen masks covering their faces and parachutes on their backs; they wait as the rear platform opens. One by one, the Army Rangers exit the plane, jumping into the wild blue yonder. They float through the sky as the narrator's voice explains that the Rangers are using an infiltration tactic known as high altitude–low opening, or HALO, to approach enemy territory.

The next screenshot shows several Rangers exiting a Blackhawk helicopter. They rappel out of the helicopter down a large rope (known as fast roping) and land on the rooftop of a building. They then line up in stack formation, one behind another. The team leader steps out of formation to place a shape charge (a plastic explosive shaped to direct the blast inward) on the entry point door handle. He turns his head as he presses the remote-control button, igniting the

1

blasting cap. The shape charge explodes, and the door blows inward. The Rangers make entry and move throughout the structure, visually confirming and surgically shooting all the 3-D enemy-combatant targets.

The Rangers continue to engage the 3-D targets throughout the building, moving from top to bottom. When the Rangers reach the bottom floor, they stop at the doorway leading out of the structure. The team leader utilizes his whisper microphone (a microphone sensor attached to the throat enabling the user to communicate at a whisper) as the narrator explains that the commando is contacting headquarters for extraction. The sound of helicopters is heard in the distance, and before long, several Blackhawk are hovering over the Rangers' location. The Ranger nearest to the exit, tosses out a smoke grenade to verify to the pilots that the landing zone is secure for extraction. The squad of Rangers moves out to board the copter on the signal of their team leader. Suddenly 3-D targets pop up. As quickly as the targets appear, the special aviation gunner drops them with machine-gun fire. The Rangers load into the copter. Now safely some distance in the air, the army commandos have pulled off another successful training exercise. Just when Ronnie thinks things are over, the building explodes in the distance.

The TV screen fades to black. An army recruiter sits back in his chair with a wide grin on his face.

"That's the best of the best. It doesn't get any more action packed than the Airborne Rangers, Ronnie my boy!"

Ronnie Slay has just graduated from college with a degree in political science. He doesn't know what direction he wants to take in life. Ronnie knows he doesn't want to work for some lousy corporation for a lousy salary in a backstabbing environment. So, Ronnie decides to serve his country and visits his local military recruiting office to check out what the service has to offer him.

When he arrives at the US Armed Forces center, he checks out each branch of the military. He doesn't choose the coast guard, because he would be stuck in the States; Ronnie wants to see the world. He does not choose the air force, because he doesn't want to experience combat from afar. Ronnie does not choose the marines, because he understands marines are considered Uncle Sam's bastard children. The marines are given very small budgets compared to the other military branches and get the army's hand-me-down equipment. Ronnie doesn't choose the navy, because their uniforms look sissified. Even though the navy has the SEAL teams, the SEALs still must wear a silly Popeye-style uniform. Also, in Ronnie's opinion, Navy SEALs is marines with the shit kicked out of them. Not to mention, SEAL teams[2] have only been around since the 1960s, so Ronnie considers SEALs the new kids on the block in the special operations community.

The US Army winds up being his military branch of choice. Ronnie understands that everybody around the world recognizes the term *GI* (government issue). The wide-eyed college grad now finds himself looking around the army recruitment office at posters of the different army combat units, impressed by the Airborne Ranger poster.

---

[2] Former president John F. Kennedy authorized the formation of the Navy SEALs in 1962.

After watching the promotional video earlier about Rangers, Ronnie is now dead set on becoming an army commando.

"So, I'll be doing that kind of stuff when I join the Rangers?" Ronnie Slay asks.

The college grad can't stop staring at the Ranger tab[3] displayed on Sergeant First Class[4] Huey's right shoulder.

The army recruiter views Ronnie Slay as a fat catfish ready to bite—hook, line, and sinker—on his closing pitch to enlist his next recruit into the army. Ronnie is just another number the aggressive recruiter needs if he wants to remain in the army.

"You bet your ass you'll be doing shit like that and much more—I promise you, kid."

Sergeant First Class Huey is a dark-green Ranger,[5] with several years of combat and special operations experience to his credit. After spending more than a decade serving in the Ranger Bats and suffering from combat-exhaustion issues, he was offered a recruiter slot and didn't hesitate to jump on the opportunity.

"Your first stop will be Officer Candidate School at Fort Benning, Georgia."

Ronnie has no idea what the recruiter is saying but decides to give the impression that he understands to save face.

"Then you'll go up the street to Chapel Hill for OIAT."

---

[3] Symbol of the army's elite commando leadership course, a.k.a. Ranger School.

[4] Army term for an enlisted service member with the rank of E-7.

[5] Army term for a Ranger of color.

Ronnie, unfamiliar with military lingo, is obviously lost. "What's OIAT, Sarg?"

Sergeant Huey presses his lips tightly together in frustration, because it's disrespectful to Huey to be called anything other than sergeant. Especially coming from a college puke.

"Officer Infantry Advanced Training, and don't call me fucking *Sarg* again!"

Huey slams a clinched fist on the top of his desk after chewing out the young recruit, results that Huey suffers from mental injury or combat exhaustion that he now takes meds for.

"I'm not a piece of meat! I'm a noncommissioned officer. You will refer to me as *sergeant*—is that clear?"

Ronnie doesn't hesitate to agree with the irate recruiter. "Clear, sir!"

Now, Ronnie doesn't know whether to get down and give Huey twenty or look for the nearest exit and rush out of the recruiting office for his own safety.

Sergeant First Class Huey stands up very slowly before speaking again. "You go to OIAT and call those drill sergeants *sarg*, not only will they slap the shit out of you; they will take pleasure in making your life a living hell."

Sergeant Huey walks behind Ronnie's chair as he continues to explain what Ronnie's life will consist of in the coming months after he begins army training. He explains that Ronnie will get a two-week break before reporting to jump school. Ronnie will remain at Fort Benning to attend jump school for a period of three weeks.

Sergeant Huey tells Ronnie that if he doesn't break any bones, he'll graduate jump school, earning his paratrooper qualification badge, his silver wings. The recruiter says Ronnie will report to the Third Ranger Regiment for RIP. Huey notices the look of confusion on Ronnie Slays' face, so he gives him the layman's explanation.

"RIP is the acronym for Ranger Indoctrination Program; it's designed to find out if you have what it takes to become an Airborne Ranger.

"If you ask me, RIP is some harassment shit the army came up with to break your will and provide entertainment to the Ranger instructors, because they're a bunch of psychos who get off on watching people suffer at their hands."

Huey tells Ronnie that if he should prove to have what it takes and is selected to go through Ranger School, he'll be given a start date. Huey makes it a point to tell Ronnie that Ranger School is one of the toughest military courses on earth and that service members have died trying to earn the Ranger tab.

Ronnie displays an uncomfortable smile as he listens to Huey's explanation. He doesn't retain much, except for the part about service members dying in their attempts to earn the Ranger tab.

Huey wraps up his explanation with his next recruit by telling him that if he should pass the commando course, he will be placed on covert missions around the world, against some of the most hostile forces seeking to destroy what the United States stands for.

"So, when do you want to start your journey to earn the black beret, young gun?"

Ronnie is so fired up, he doesn't hesitate to jump to his feet, shouting, "As soon as possible, Sarg!"

Realizing what he just did, Ronnie quickly corrects himself.

"I mean *sergeant*!"

Sergeant Huey cracks a stern grin, displaying a gold crown on one of his teeth.

"That's what I'm talking about. I'll make a Ranger out of you yet."

Soldier Boy

Currently it's midnight in the basement of Georgia International Airport. Ronnie, along with other recruits from around the country, has been in the basement for hours, waiting to be transported to Fort Benning to begin basic training.

After sitting and stewing in the basement of the airport for most of the day, Ronnie begins to have second thoughts about joining the army. He reflects to the day he told his family, his friends, and his high school sweetheart, Tammy Scott, he was joining the military. His friends couldn't believe he would do something as drastic as joining the military when he could make a fortune working for his father.

Tammy was devastated when Ronnie joined the military instead of marrying her. Deep in his heart, Ronnie knew marrying Tammy was a pipe dream. He felt he was too young to settle down and be a good husband to her. He was like a young lion, seeking to roam free and explore the world.

Tammy was a very attractive girl; half the guys in Helena would jump at the chance to strike up a relationship with her. Ronnie, deep down inside, is afraid of commitment. Most of all, he is afraid of failing to give Tammy a happily ever after.

Ronnie Slay finds it ironic that he is willing to put his life on the line to defend his country but is afraid to put his heart on the line for the only girl he has ever loved.

The other woman in his life who was devastated by his decision to join the military was his mom. Mrs. Slay begged her only son not to follow through with joining the army. The opposite could be said about Mr. Slay; he supports whatever decisions his son makes. He relates to his son's desire to become his own man, walking to his own drumbeat in life.

Ronnie explains to his mom that the United States hasn't been involved in a military conflict since the Vietnam War. Although the Middle East is unstable, he doesn't feel the environment over there will affect the American way of life. Ronnie does his best to reassure his mon that she doesn't have to worry about losing only child to America's foreign policies.

Ronnie's moment of reflection comes to an end as the doors to the room in the basement swing open. Stone-faced army sergeants bark out orders for all the recruits to get to their feet and move their asses into the hallway. Ronnie and the other recruits are hustled onto a military bus, which transports them to Fort Benning for basic training.

PANAMA

I t's 1989, and the year unfolds with a bang. US war planes shoot down two Libyan fighters over international waters in January. In April, tens of thousands of Chinese students take over Beijing's Tiananmen Square, protesting for democracy in China.

Several other events happened during 1989, but toward the end of the year, the president of the United States announces on network news that he is authorizing the invasion of Panama to safeguard the lives of US citizens from forces loyal to dictator and strongman Noriega. First Lieutenant Slay is the intelligence officer on a two-man long-range reconnaissance patrol (LRRP) scout team; First Lieutenant Hunter is the scout sniper.

Their mission is to go out and conduct a strategic reconnaissance mission of areas of interest to pinpoint the whereabouts of Noriega's private jet, to prevent the renegade dictator from fleeing apprehension and prosecution by the United States of America for drug smuggling across international waters.

Slay and Hunter fast rope into the jungles of Panama.

Ronnie thinks, *We're going live downrange. From here on, it's kill or be killed.*

As he and Tony start their stealthy trek toward Noriega's compound, they use night vision goggles as they move into a two-man, 360-degree security overwatch formation.[6] They do this to ward off a possible enemy assault.

They communicate with each other utilizing code names to counter enemy radio interception measures.

"Snake Eyes, how you feel?"

"Besides feeling like I'm in a freaking sauna, I'm good to go, brah."

Lieutenant Slay reviews the map showing coordinates to their objective before they move out.

"Okay, we're moving out in that direction, brah."

Lieutenant Hunter scans from left to right, being conscious to move the barrel of his MP5 machinegun in the same direction. The machinegun is Hunter's secondary weapon; his primary weapon is a Barrett .50-caliber sniper rifle, capable of killing enemy two miles away.

Lieutenant Slay is equipped with an AK-47 assault rifle fitted with a grenade launcher and silencer. His secondary weapon is a Desert Eagle handgun, also fitted with a silencer. Both commandos have M1 combat knives,[7] garrote chokers,[8] combat-load Alice military backpacks, and the latest communication devices for their mission. Slay

---

[6] This type of security formation gives combatants 180-degree sectors of fire.

[7] These knives double as bayonets.

[8] This weapon is used for silent kills, by slicing through the flesh to the bone.

activates his satellite phone to check in with the southern (JSOC) officers assigned to their mission.

"Anaconda, this is Ghost Recon Two. Have arrived at the ORP."[9]

"Proceed to objective as schedule. copy?"

"roger that, Ghost Recon Two out." Ronnie replies.

"Update command when you have a visual on objective, out here." JSOC command says.

Slay powers down the satellite phone.

"Snake Eyes, we're hot."

Slay double-checks the map coordinates before giving the signal to Hunter to move out.

Lieutenant Hunter does a hasty visual scan of the jungle before stepping off. Their mission is in support of Operation Just Cause. On December 17, the US president ordered more than twenty-five thousand troops to invade the Panamanian regime, which strongman dictator Noriega is barely holding on to.

Once Hunter and Slay locate and confirm the position of Noriega's private jet, they are to report back to JSOC, which will deploy a direct-action team to blow up the aircraft. Hunter gets to his feet, on the alert. He brings up rear security while Slay navigates them to the objective using land-navigation methods.

Slay and Hunter can see the outline of Eighty-Second Airborne paratroopers in the twilight sky, descending to the ground, ready to unleash death and destruction upon enemy forces.

US marines approach from the beachhead. The best of

---

[9] Objective rallying point.

the best are storming Panama, including First and Second Ranger Bats.,[10] Army Special Forces,[11] Navy SEALs, and Detachment Delta.[12] The mission of Detachment Delta is to rescue an American citizen who has been locked up in a Panamanian prison for broadcasting anti–Manuel Noriega propaganda throughout the Central American nation. Execution orders have been issued to prison guards to kill the American at the first sign of any type of a rescue attempt.

Slay and Hunter could call in close air support (CAS) to prevent a large enemy force from overrunning them, as well as provide them with a window of opportunity to escape from being captured.

After an hour and a half of patrolling, Slay and Hunter find themselves on top of a ridgeline overlooking a compound. Dawn is slowly approaching, so the cover of darkness will soon be gone. Slay appraises the area and likes it as their position to operate from. "Okay, let's set up our OAO[13] here, Tony."

They drop their Alice packs and conceal them in the jungle foliage behind the OAO. Hunter takes up a position that will give him the best line of sight on the compound below, to provide sniper support for Slays recon.

Before heading out, Slay sets up early-warning devices at the likely avenues of enemy approach. He then sets up

---

[10] Abbreviation for US Army Ranger battalions.

[11] Green Berets.

[12] The US Army's mysterious Delta Force operatives.

[13] Objective area of operations.

Claymore mines[14] with trip wires, seven meters past the early-warning devices, in case the enemy discovers and disarms the early-warning devices. The final security measure Slay and Hunter take is to create passwords to identify friend from foe.

Slay double-checks the gear needed to recon the compound below. Once satisfied, he moves out and disappears under the jungle's triple canopy. Hunter loses sight of his partner and now must rely on GPS technology to track Slay.

First Lieutenant Slay makes his way through the dense jungle. The humid air envelops him, weighing down on him like a wet blanket, making it difficult to breathe normally. His thoughts begin to race; he fights to stay focused on the goal of the mission. It's his first real mission, and, truth is, the commando is scared, not so much of being killed but of failing to accomplish the mission. Slay knows this isn't Key West.[15] He understands this isn't training. He thinks, *All right, this is the real shit. I need to get my head out of my ass, or I will find it in a body bag. What happens if the fucking plane isn't here? Do we hurry up and wait in this fucking blazing-hot jungle?*

The jungle foliage begins to thin out, and the compounds wall comes into view. Slay stops to contact Hunter, to confirm the sniper has a good visual of his position before continuing the recon. Slay goes to one knee near the compound wall.

---

[14] Packed with steel balls and C-4 explosive, a Claymore mine will turn a person to bits of flesh and blood.

[15] Location where special operations forces learn the craft of their trade.

Hunter confirms Slays' position from the blinking strobe reflectors located on the front and back of Slays' battle dress top, visible only to Hunter's specialized optics.

Slay keeps battling negative thoughts, envisioning being murdered by an enemy combatant. But he falls back on his military training, which proves to be stronger than his negative mindset. Despite his combat jitters, Slay knows he won't hesitate to kill the enemy, be they man, woman, or child.

Slay moves out in a slow and deliberate manner, scanning his immediate front, from left to right, for enemy movement.

Back on top of the ridgeline, Hunter is also scanning for enemy movement. He spots Slay's strobe reflectors in the distance. The threat of dawn is approaching, and soon they both will have to stow their night vision goggles in their carrying cases. Finally, Hunter spots an enemy soldier emerging from a doorway of the compound.

The un-sub,[16] armed with an M16A1 rifle slung across his shoulder in a nonchalant manner, is enjoying a cigarette.

"Hansel, this is Snake Eyes. Over."

Slay stops in his tracks and drops to one knee.

"This is Hansel. Send your traffic."

"Hostile, moving fifty meters to your right flank. Wearing an OD[17] uniform. He appears to be on guard duty or patrol, but he's not taking it serious. He's paying more attention to the motherfucking cancer stick in his mouth."

---

[16] Unknown subject.

[17] Olive drab.

Slay grins to himself over Hunter's style of radio procedure.

"Stand by while I do another visual of the compound."

"Roger—standing by."

Hunter doesn't find any other threats, but he does observe the current threat closing the distance to Lieutenant Slay. The un-sub arrives at an observation post, sits down, and leans back in a chair. He continues to enjoy his cigarette.

"Hansel, this is Snake Eyes."

"Go ahead, Snake Eyes," Slay says.

"No other threats spotted. Our carefree un-sub is fifty meters to your left front. Take him out and proceed east to the compound wall.

"Once there, follow it to the right. You'll come to a door left ajar by our friend. How copy?"

"Good copy, Snake Eyes. Over and out."

Slay silently stalks toward the un-sub. This will be his first kill. He knew this day would come at some point during his military career. But he figured his first kill would be from afar, using firearms. Never in a million years did he expect to make his first kill up close and personal with his bare hands. Negative thoughts return.

What if this guy is stronger than me? What if he turns the tables, and I'm the one who gets killed?

The sun is steadily rising. Soon the compound will be crawling with more threats, complicating the mission. Ronnie knows he doesn't have the luxury of second-guessing himself. He scans his left front to see if he can spot the threat, and he catches a glimpse of the glow of the cigarette.

Shit! Hunter wasn't joking. This guy is real freaking close.

Ronnie circles around to approach the threat from the

rear for a backdoor ambush. As he closes in on the guard, Slay removes his garrote. He gets within arm's reach. His heart is racing a million miles an hour. Ronnie is sure this guy can hear his heart pounding. His mouth is dry. He desperately needs to clear his throat but can't risk being heard.

Lieutenant Slay feels like he is frozen in time. The unsuspecting soldier blows out cigarette smoke. Slay inhales some of the secondhand smoke as he wraps his choker around the guard's neck. Lieutenant Slay tightens it, cutting into the guard's throat to the bone. The guard's blood sprays all over Slays' neck and chin, as well as his hands. The guard is dead before the cigarette smoke dissipates into the air. Slay straightens the dead soldier's corpse in the chair to give the appearance the dead man is alert and on guard.

Slay makes his way along the compound wall to the doorway. He arrives at the door and slowly pushes it open to find a walkway leading to a secondary enclosure. Hunter informs Slay he has just twenty minutes to complete his reconnaissance before sunrise. He adds that if Lieutenant Slay isn't back by that time, he will request a CAS mission to level the compound, figuring that Lieutenant Slay has been captured or killed. This is standard procedure for covert operators should their mission be compromised, to avoid complicating the military operations occurring in other areas of Panama.

Slay makes his way to the inner structure. He enters to discover Noriega's private plane inside.

Slay removes a camcorder from his equipment carrier and begins recording his findings. He comes across another set of sliding panel doors and opens them to discover an unimproved road airstrip. Slay is sure plenty of drug-smuggling operations have gone down here on a regular basis. The airstrip is concealed by the jungle's triple canopy, making it impossible to spot the airstrip and hangar via satellite. Now Slay understands the need for such a large guard force; they not only protect Noriega's plane but also keep the jungle foliage cleared away from the airstrip on a regular basis.

Fifteen minutes have passed; it's time for Slay to wrap up his recon and return to the OAO. Slay secures the hangar door, so as not to draw suspicion from other guards later during the day. Slay arrives back at the OAO.

Hunter renders a challenge. "Halt!"

"Eleven."

"Bang, bang."

Slay can advance into the OAO. Hunter emerges from his sniper position draped in his camouflage ghillie suit.

"Welcome back, brah. I was ready to call in the big guns on your ass."

Slay gives Hunter an exhausted grin. "If you thought you could get rid of me that easy, you're sadly mistaken, brah."

They both laugh together quietly. Slay removes his equipment carrier to retrieve the camcorder. He and Hunter disappear into their concealed position.

They watch the video of Slay's recon.

Hunter interrupts the video session. "Can I ask you a question, Ronnie?"

"Do you have to at this very moment? Can it wait?"

"I'll make it quick, brah. What's it like to kill somebody?"

Slay is at a loss for words, his face blank.

"Hey, brah, you okay?" Tony snaps his fingers in Ronnie's direction.

"Huh? Sorry, Tony. You want to know what it's like to kill someone?"

"Yeah, brah—what did it feel like?"

Ronnie takes a short breath before responding. "Man … I could feel his energy leaving his body when I wrapped my garrote around his neck and tightened it. His blood sprayed all over my hands and neck, and then he was like a dead fish.

"I don't think killing someone up close and personal compares to doing it from afar, brah."

Eerily, Hunter hangs on every word coming out of Ronnie's mouth, like an apprentice hanging on every word of a master teaching him secrets of the trade he must come to master.

"Wow, that's deep, brah. Did you take a trophy?"

Ronnie shrugs in response to Hunter's inquiry. "What do you mean, did I take a trophy?"

"You know, like cutting off an ear or a finger of the dead guy for a trophy."

"Are you serious, brah? Hell no. I killed the guy and moved out to complete the mission."

"Okay, chill, brah. I was just curious. I thought you'd heard the war stories about how the Hellhound[18] vets would take body parts of enemy combatants they killed as trophies. It's like a rite of passage or something."

"Tony, I have no interest in carrying around the rotting flesh of dead people. Not to mention, the enemy would have

---

[18] Nickname for Army Rangers.

no problem tracking me with rotting flesh reeking from my gear. Doesn't make much sense to me, brah."

"I'm not going to lie, brah: I'm looking forward to the day I get to snuff me a motherfucker during this op."

As Slay gets up to retrieve his laptop from his Alice pack, he thinks, *I see why snipers are considered a weird bunch.*

He returns to upload the data from the camcorder onto the laptop's secured network and send it to JSOC.

Hunter conducts another visual recon of the compound to find out what's unfolding down there. Slay completes the video upload for the JSOC commanders to review. Headquarters confirms the delivery of the data, congratulating Slay and Hunter on a job well done. Now that the objective is confirmed, command instructs Slay and Hunter to remain out of sight and continue to monitor the compound, maintaining radio silence until the assault team destroys November Papa Joliet.[19] Then, and only then, are they to break radio silence to verify the same. Command is sending Navy SEALs to the compound to destroy Noriega's plane.

---

[19] Code name for Noriega's private jet.

GREEN-FACED FROGMEN

S lay makes his way to the observation post to inform
Hunter of the latest developments. It's Hunter's turn
to fill Slay in on the new developments unfolding on the
compound. He tells Slay the dead guy was discovered half
an hour ago. Patrols are being conducted on a regular
basis. Also, Lieutenant Hunter believes the guard force has
acquired a crew-served heavy machine gun.

Slay rubs his chin after hearing Hunter's situation report.
A heavy machine gun will complicate the assault force's
effort to destroy Noriega's plane. Slay feels it's his fault this
present problem has developed on the objective. He should
have hidden the body of the guard after killing him, instead
of propping him up in the chair, giving the impression that
all was well. If he'd hidden the body, perhaps the rest of the
guard force might have thought he went AWOL.[20]

Slay wipes sweat from his forehead as he brainstorms
what to do about the potential presence of a crew-served
weapon that is capable of shredding the assault team to
hamburger.

---

[20]

For Lieutenants Slay and Hunter, it is a time of terror, because they believe a heavy machine gun might be lurking somewhere in the compound below. Unknown to both commandos, hardened Panamanian infantry killers known as Battalion 2000 have been dispatched to Noriega's compound to reinforce the Panamanian guard force with a .50-caliber heavy machine gun after the corpse of the guard Lieutenant Slay took out earlier was discovered.

Slay and Hunter know how to stop the terror before it happens, but their hands are tied. They've been given orders to maintain radio silence until the assault force made up of Navy SEALs has completed the mission of taking out Noriega's private jet. If Slay and Hunter maintain radio silence, Battalion 2000 will indeed shred the assault force without hesitation.

Hunter suggests that they contact JSOC anyway, before the assault team is deployed, to report the possibility of a heavy machine gun. Ronnie agrees to make the call.

At dusk, the jungle becomes so dark that they can't see their hands in front of their faces, even if they snap their fingers. The only noises they can hear are the sounds of jungle wildlife and the random rifle fire that comes from the guard force due to their paranoia after finding one of their own dead in their backyard.

The time now is Zulu hour—midnight in civilian terms. The jungle has a strange silence to it; most of the guards appear to be retiring for the night. Slay and Hunter utilize their night vision goggles again to keep a vigilant watch for the crew-served weapon believed to be somewhere in the compound below.

After being briefed by JSOC commanders with the intel

from Lieutenants Slay and Hunter's recon of the compound, the assault force made up of Navy SEALs is inserted into the area, parachuting four miles outside the compound. Unfortunately, their received information didn't include mention of the potential crew-served weapon at the objective.

With their specialized optics, Slay and Hunter spot blinking strobe reflectors north of their position.

"Ronnie, do you see what I see?" Lieutenant Hunter whispers.

"You got to be fucking kidding me."

"Why would the assault team approach the objective using the freaking road, Ronnie?"

"Guess we'll soon find out if there is a freaking crew-served weapon for sure, huh?"

The silent jungle erupts with the sound of small arms fire.

"Shit!"

"Those guys are being cut to pieces!"

"We can't stand by and do nothing!" Hunter pleads with Slay.

Lieutenant Slay breaks radio silence and contacts JSOC, informing command of the events unfolding at the objective. Slay is told he has disobeyed a direct order to maintain radio silence. The assault team can deal with hostile fire and will push through to execute and accomplish their mission. Slay is ordered not to break radio silence unless he is contacting command with a sitrep.[21]

"Shit! Those pencil dicks have their heads up their ass!"

"What did they say, brah?"

---

[21] Situation report.

"Fucking maintain radio silence!"

"Blah, blah, blah."

Hunter and Slay turn their attention back to the compound and observe the SEALs on the airstrip in a V-wedge[22] formation. Machine-gun fire erupts to the left flank of the SEAL team. Tracer rounds light up the jungle like deadly candlelight, flying, followed by full-metal-jacket rounds racing toward their targets. Slay and Hunter watch in horror as the SEALs are mowed down like ducks in a shooting gallery.

"Still going to maintain radio silence, brah?"

"Fuck this! I'm not going to stand by and watch this massacre! Fuck radio silence."

Instead of contacting JSOC, Slay contacts Special Operations Forces Command (SOFC), which oversees JSOC, to request that First Bat deploy Hellhounds to reinforce their objective site. His request is approved without delay.

---

[22] A infantry patrol tactical formation.

HELLHOUNDS

Quickly, Slay and Hunter change into their assault gear and go over their plan of attack.

"Tony, set up an overwatch position giving you the best sector of fire to provide the best sniper fire for me, brah. We got to find that fucking machine-gun position and take it out before First Bat arrives. Cut down anything that comes within fifty meters of me."

"Got you covered, brah."

Slay pauses before heading out. "Guess you're going to find out what it's like to kill someone sooner than you thought, brah."

Lieutenant Hunter displays his trademark smile. "Let's do this."

Lieutenant Slay makes his way through the jungle, listening to the screams of wounded service members. He double-checks his weapon to ensure he has a fully loaded clip, with one round in the chamber. The screams of the wounded become louder.

Lieutenant Slay slows down and drops to a knee to conduct a hasty sweep of the general area. He spots a figure about forty meters to his front. Without drawing attention to himself, Slay gets into a prone position and begins to low crawl toward the figure.

About fifteen meters from the un-sub, Slay realizes the un-sub is using a knife to slice at the hand of one of the wounded SEALs. The un-sub pauses to prop his assault rifle against a palm tree and then resumes slicing at the sailor's hand. He's attempting to amputate the sailor's ring finger.

Slay aims his assault rifle's laser sight at the un-sub. When the dual red light hits the Panamanian's hand, he immediately stops cutting. The soldier jumps to his feet and attempts to recover his weapon. Lieutenant Slay blows his brains out with a single shot. He makes his way toward the sailor's location. The SEAL is relieved to have been rescued.

"Who the hell are you?"

"Lieutenant Slay, First Ranger Bat. Glad I could help."

The sailor clutches his right hand in pain. "Chief Petty Officer Collins. Yeah, thanks for getting that maggot off me. He was trying to cut off my NSWC[23] ring."

Gunfire mixed with screams erupts once again. Ronnie helps Chief Collins to his feet. He asks Collins if he has any other wounds. Collins tells Ronnie his right leg was grazed during the ambush. The sailor veteran tells Ronnie how many men are on the assault team. He doesn't know how many of them are wounded. Ronnie asks Collins why his team chose to approach the objective using the road. Collins says that, during their mission brief, they were informed the objective was defended by a ragtag guard force. So, the team figured the road was the quickest avenue of approach

---

[23] Naval Special Warfare Command.

to get in and out swiftly. They didn't receive any intel about a crew-served weapon on the objective.

Slay and Collins move slowly through the bush. Collins uses his weak hand on Ronnie as a crutch, using his strong hand to keep his weapon at the ready to repel any attack by enemy combatants.

Collins can't recall the direction he and his team were traveling before they were ambushed. He gives Lieutenant Slay the general direction as being straight across from where he and the army commandos are currently located.

Slay lowers Chief Collins to the ground and scans the far side of the road for movement using his night vision goggles before attempting to cross the danger area. Ronnie gets a visual on the Seals' tactical strobe reflectors. He also spots enemy soldiers approaching the wounded sailors to finish them off. Unlike the US, Panama, doesn't follow the Geneva Convention agreements.[24]

"I see your men. I'm going to make my way to their position and have them link up with you over here."

Captain Slay wakes up momentarily as the Blackhawk helicopter transporting him to Hunter Army Airfield in Hinesville, Georgia, runs into some rough turbulence. Slay briefly opens his eyes to find Captain Hunter staring at him, his trademark smile on his face. Hunter grabs a headset while pointing to the headset next to Slay's head, signaling for Slay to put it on. Slay grabs the headset.

"What's up, brah?" Ronnie asks.

---

[24] A series of treaties on the treatment of civilians and prisoners of war.

"You tell me. You're the one having issues over there."

Captain Slay closes his eyes, shaking his head at Captain Hunter's comment, not wanting to admit Captain Hunter is right; he is having issues, in the form of flashbacks as he sleeps.

"Guess I must have had a nightmare or something, brah."

Captain Hunter nods in agreement. "I understand. Just don't get too caught up in the moment. I'd hate to lose you because you freaked out and fell out of the copter. How would I explain that to your parents?"

Slay and Hunter laugh out loud together.

"Finish resting, sleeping ugly. I'll wake you when we arrive at Hunter Airfield."

Ronnie folds his arms and leans back in his cargo seat to finish his nap. "Appreciate you, brah. You're all right in my book, no matter what the guys in the squad say about you."

Captain Hunter laughs out loud as he removes his headset. Captain Slay does the same. It doesn't take Slay long to drift back to sleep, finding himself back in the jungles of Panama.

Moving at a smooth rate of speed toward the wounded Navy SEALs, Slay consciously points the muzzle of his weapon in the same direction as he looks.

A figure jumps out on his right flank. Ronnie identifies that figure as an enemy combatant before letting loose with an accurate burst of full-metal-jacket rounds, tearing a huge hole in the man's chest.

Ronnie hears yelling in Spanish, followed by dead silence. Hunter is providing accurate and deadly sniper support for the wounded SEALs until Slay can reach their location. Eventually Ronnie makes it to the other side of the unimproved road where the sailors took cover.

Five more meters in, Slay drops to one knee to scan the darkness with his night vision goggles. A lump rises in his throat as he thinks, *Lord, please let Hunter have a visual on my location.*

Slay hopes the sailors don't open fire on him, mistaking him for an enemy combatant, before he can ID himself as an ally.

"American coming your way to assist you—don't shoot!"

Slay observes the SEALs are in a 360-degree security formation.

"PSs, over here."

Slay moves in that direction to observe a green-faced SEAL peering at him from an observation post ten meters from the SEAL team's formation as a first line of defense.

ALL HELL BREAKS LOOSE

S lay slowly enters the concealed location.

"We got to get ourselves out of this shit sandwich, troops."

Lieutenant Slay is brought into the security formation, confronted with the carnage the heavy machine gun has inflicted on most of the SEAL team. One of the sailors who was fortunate enough to avoid being wounded inquiries about how Lieutenant Slay wound up in their presence. Slay explains that he is one of the two-man recon team that gathered intel for the assault mission. When it becomes apparent that Slays' team failed to report the heavy machine gun in their sitrep, tempers flare. Slay and an irate SEAL are separated by other sailors.

The navy officer regains his composure. Once hostilities are over, the navy commando turns his attention to how they can get out of Panama with their lives. Lieutenant Slay informs the SEALs of Senior Chief Collins's location. The majority of the team links up with Collins on the other side of the road while Slay and the naval officer remain in the concealed position. They plan to take the fight to the enemy by manning the crew-served weapon.

"I'm Captain Nelson, by the way."

They shake hands. They hear the sound of helicopters in the distance. Both commandos turn their attention to the approaching copters.

"What the hell is going on now?" Captain Nelson asks.

"It's my guys."

"It's who?"

"First Ranger Bat."

Both commandos take the opportunity to launch a surprise attack to take out the .50-caliber machine gun.

The 160th Night Stalker helicopters carrying the Ranger assault team are escorted by two highly technical Cobra attack copters. The first copter banks to the left, the second to the right. Both pilots fire flares to light up the jungle below to expose the enemy to their deadly payloads. The compound erupts with small arms fire in the direction of the copters. In response, the copters fire Hellfire missiles, which slam into the compound and explode.

A huge ball of fire rises into the Panamanian night sky. The pilots utilize night vision technology to establish their sectors of fire on the enemy and to identify friendlies. They observe the strobe reflectors on the wounded SEALs, Lieutenants Slay and Hunter, and Captain Nelson.

By radio, Ronnie requests the CH-46 copter pilot to carry the Ranger assault team to the rear of the hangar inside the compound. Hellhounds fast rope out of the transport copter.

"I have a visual on the mother bird laying her eggs, Hansel. Copy?"

"That's a good copy, Silver Surfer. Be advised we're going into the hornets' nest. Copy?"

"Good copy, Hansel."

"Be advised: heavy machine gun located at three o'clock from your location."

"Let's fry some bad guys. Over and out."

"Roger. Out."

On the ground, the Rangers move toward the hangar to locate Noriega's jet. Slay and Captain Nelson race toward the heavy machine gun's position before it can be used against the assault team. Both Slay and Nelson go to one knee and scan the dark, using their night vision goggles.

Slay spots the crew-served weapon being moved by four enemy soldiers. "Slay spots the crew-served weapon being moved by four enemy soldiers. "Jackpot."

"I have a visual on our target,"

Nelson responds.

"Follow me."

Nelson removes a satchel charge containing Composition C-4 explosives from his equipment pack and preps it before moving out. Slay checks his magazine, ensuring it is at full capacity. They head out in a three o'clock direction, encountering no enemy resistance. They make entry through the front compound doors, being sure to clear the corners in their sectors of fire.

The assault team destroys Noriega's private jet by firing a projectile into its fuel sludge. Slay and Nelson open fire, killing the machine-gun crew. Nelson approaches the weapon while Slay provides cover fire. Nelson places the satchel charge under the machine gun, sets the fuse, and races back to Lieutenant Slay's location.

"You better get your head down, Lieutenant. There's about to be a large—"

Before Nelson can finish his statement, a huge explosion erupts, filling the night jungle sky with a small orange ball of fire.

The assault team exits from the hangar to stand by for pickup. The assault team leader uses a secured radio to request evacuation. He is instructed to locate Lieutenants Slay and Hunter, plus the Navy SEALs, for pickup as well.

TIME-TRAVEL AGENTS

Lieutenants Slay and Hunter take seats at the rear of the copter.

"We made it, brother."

"That shit was crazy, brah. Your sniping was second to none."

"Those SEALs got shot up pretty bad, huh?" Tony asks.

"Yeah, but most of them made it out in one piece. Their commanding officer recorded the grid coordinates for the location of their dead to be recovered later."

The copter crew chief approaches carrying a satellite phone in his hand. "Which one of you is Lieutenant Slay?"

Ronnie identifies himself.

"You have a call from JSOC, Lieutenant." The crew chief hands the phone to Slay.

Ronnie's eyes are the size of silver dollars at this point.

"Lieutenant Slay, this is Colonel Hawkins. You and your team are going on a covert operation."

Hunter listens very intently to Ronnie's conversation after overhearing the words *covert mission*.

"Your team will be dropped off in Panama City to be picked up for this assignment."

"What kind of mission, sir?"

"You'll be given details at your brief. Until then, you and your team link up with elements of the Eighty-Second Airborne Division at Revolution Avenue. They will escort you to the designated pickup point to be taken to your briefing. Is that clear, Lieutenant?"

"Clear, sir."

"Good luck out here."

"Roger. Out."

Hunter removes his bandana, a look of concern mixed with excitement on his face.

"What was that all about, Ronnie?"

"We've been assigned another mission by JSOC, brah."

"Just what we need, another cluster fuck mission." Hunter replies.

"What do you think we're up against Ronnie?"

Lieutenant Slay rubs his forehead before replying to Lieutenant Hunter's question.

"All I can tell you is we are to link up with a squad from the 82nd Airborne Division to be escorted to the DPP."[25]

"Are you serious? When the Eighty-Deuce is on the loose, friendly fire incidents follow. We're supposed to place our safety in the hands of those yahoos?"

Ronnie rubs his forehead. "I feel your pain, Tony. Unfortunately, those are our marching orders."

This takes Slay back to Ranger School, which seems like a lifetime ago. He recalls how exhausted he was every day during training, like he is now. He remembers how the Ranger instructors told him and the other trainees they

---

[25] Designated pickup point.

would have days like this in real combat situations, unable to think straight, the body wanting to quit. But the mind must override the pain of the body. They must stay strong to complete the mission at all cost.

Instead of heading back to JSOC for much-needed sack time and a good meal, Slay and Hunter are off to a destination unknown.

Ronnie thinks, *Guess I pissed off the wrong people at JSOC when I broke radio silence. I'd do it again in a heartbeat to save the lives of my brothers-in-arms.*

It's by design that Slay, and Hunter know very little about their next mission. The mission is a black operations assignment, the highest level of secretive covert mission undertaken by special operations forces. Operatives have little to no chain of command or support. Should a problem arise and the mission be compromised, the operatives will be left out to dry and will most likely be killed by their capt ors.

This black operations mission is connected to an alien device that enables time travel. Slay and Hunter will be kept in the dark regarding the facts about this asset that is not indigenous to planet Earth. This asset can alter past, present, and future circumstances in a positive or negative manner.

The CH-46 copter hovers over a building. The crew chief gives the signal for Slay and Hunter to exit the copter using a fast rope. They land on the roof of an abandoned hotel. The copter is gone as fast as it arrived, leaving Slay and Hunter on the roof.

Hunter's face displays a so-what-do-we-do-now expression. "So, where's our raspberry-beret escort, brah?"

Lieutenant Slay looks irritated. "Tony, you have to learn how to play nice with others. The Eighty-Deuce is America's guard of honor and our protectors. They will make sure we get to the pickup point safely."

"I'll try to play nice, but if one of those clowns points their weapon in the general direction of either one of us, I'm going to make sure we're not friendly fire vics, brah," Hunter says, tapping his weapon.

"Fair enough, brah, but remember: most of these troops are a bunch of kids straight out of high school, with little to no combat experience."

"Speaking of the devilish, insane clown posse, they're approaching our position at twelve o'clock."

Lieutenant Slay fires up a flare using a star cluster canister to identify their location to the paratroopers. Shortly, the airborne platoon makes its way to the rooftop and joins Slay and Hunter. The platoon sergeant introduces himself. He has a typical name from small-town USA. He pulls out his map, already prepped with the grid coordinates.

Hunter maintains his position at his observation post and overhears some of the paratroopers complaining to Sergeant Wilson.

"This is bullshit, Sarg!"

"Why do we have to miss out on all the real action to escort two freak' in Rangers?"

"Yeah, I thought Rangers lead the way and all that good shit."

"Can't they lead the way to wherever it is they need to go?"

Hunter leave his position to approach the troopers, and Slay moves to intercept his brother-in-arms.

"Stand down, brah. We're on another level."

"Let's get this mission over with and get some much needed R&R."

Hunter nods in agreement and returns to his position.

"Is your man okay?"

"Yeah, he's a little on the tense side. We just came off a hairy mission hours ago. You can relate, right?"

"Yeah, I sure can."

Lieutenants Slay and Hunter recheck their grid coordinates with the paratroopers before heading out. They hear explosions and automatic fire in the distance throughout the night, but they don't encounter any enemy resistance as they make their way down through war-torn Panama City. After patrolling for about five miles, the point man signals the paratroopers to halt. Sergeant Wilson makes his way toward the point man.

"What do you have, Corporal?"

"Sarg, I believe this is the DPP. According to the map, we will find a huge mud lake at the rear of that building at four o'clock."

Slay, Hunter, and Sergeant Wilson come together to compare notes to see if they have any special instructions to pass on.

"This is where we part ways, Lieutenant. Been a pleasure working with you and Lieutenant Hunter, sir."

"Same here, Sergeant. Your troops have been nothing but professional. By any chance, did you get the name of the unit that will be picking us up?"

"No, sir. I was told little to nothing. Need-to-know type shit."

"Okay, Sergeant. You and your troops be safe out there in the bush."

The two military leaders shake hands. The paratroopers move out, and once again Slay and Hunter are alone.

Daybreak is approaching slowly; Slay and Hunter hole up in an abandoned hotel, playing the hurry-up-and-wait game. Their patience wears thin.

"Ronnie, this is a fucked-up situation, brah."

Hunter shakes his head.

"Think about it, we get this mission at the last minute, and we have no idea who the hell is picking us up?

The whole thing is shady if you ask me, brah."

"I agree, brah, but we volunteered for this type of shit. In fact, our dumb asses volunteered three times if you think about it."[26]

---

[26] Special forces troops are three-time volunteers, volunteering first for military service in one of the four branches (including the coast guard), then for jump school, and finally for special operations skills.

SUITS

Hunter gives Slay a blank stare and then returns to what he was doing earlier.

"I reviewed my notes," Slay says. "They state we will be picked up by copter."

"Does it mention who's doing the picking up?"

"Naw. Sorry, brah."

"Something else is bugging the hell out of me, brah."

Slay shakes his head, indicating he doesn't want to hear what Hunter has to say. Small arms fire and explosions erupt around Slay and Hunter's location. They hear vehicle engines, along with the sound of crew-served weapons being fired. It is now predawn, and instead of night vision goggles, Hunter uses binoculars to observe the events unfolding in the streets below.

"Hey, brah, you won't believe what's going on below."

"Let me have a look."

Panamanian Battalion 2000, a special forces troop, is locked in a fierce firefight with fellow army Rangers.

The Panamanians are firing recoil rifles mounted on two modified Toyota pickup trucks. Every time the Panamanians fire their recoil rifles, the fronts of their vehicles fly up in the air, damn near flipping over. It's a hilarious sight to Slay and Hunter.

One of the trucks explodes into flames, and the same happens to the second one. The surviving Panamanian commandos flee for their lives but are cut down by a hail of bullets fired upon them by the Silent Birds'[27] Miniguns.

The remaining enemy combatants flee in different directions but are cut down by surgical small arms fire from US Rangers concealed in the upper floors of the opposite building from Slay and Hunter.

As fast as the combat erupted, it ends. Only eerie silence remains. Voices bark out orders; someone using a bullhorn calls out for Slay and Hunter to come to the street.

"This sure 'nuff some bizarre shit, brah."

"Hell yeah."

Both Slay and Hunter laugh out loud together as they head out to the street. They come face-to-face with a Ranger field grade officer holding a bullhorn.

Both Slay, and Hurter are familiar with the major, who is from Fort Benning. This Ranger has close ties to the black operations community.

"Men, I'm your contact. My name isn't important, so don't ask."

The major isn't dressed like his subordinate Rangers; he's dressed in all-black sanitized combat fatigues.

"I am to ensure you two get to your briefing on time. Yesterday, counter communications intercepted a radio

---

[27] Silent Birds are stealth copter used by the special aviators from the Night Stalkers Regiment.

transmission indicating the Panamanians planned on kidnapping the two of you.

"Intel uncovered info about your rendezvous; SASOC[28] dispatched us to secure your location to prevent hostel from kidnapping you both."

Unbeknownst to Slay and Hunter, two dragonfly-looking copters, flown by pilots also dressed in all-black fatigues, silently hover forty feet behind and above the two unaware lieutenants.

The stealth technology these UAPs[29] are built with did not derive from planet Earth. The lieutenants are told transportation is ready to whisk them to the briefing area. To say they are surprised is an understatement.

Both Lieutenants Hunter and Slay climb aboard their respective birds, because this is protocol to prevent losing both operatives to anti-aircraft strike. Copters zoom off in the night silently. Ten miles from Panama City, Slay and Hunter observe what looks like crash site with debris scattered all over the Sarigua Desert floor below.

It isn't long before Slay and Hunter arrive at the temporary dark site known only to those currently inside it. Two individuals, dressed in the same black fatigues the pilots were wearing, escort Slay and Hunter to the doorway of a desert-camouflage tent.

Inside the tent is a man in a military uniform, with the rank of four-star general, and two officials dressed in black civilian suits, typical apparel for government officials. The

[28] South American Special Operations Command.
[29] Unidentified aerial phenomena.

three men are going over a terrain model of the operational area where Slay and Hunter are to conduct their mission.

"Please, Lieutenant Slay, Lieutenant Hunter, come in. Welcome to nowhere. I'm General Hopkins."

Slay and Hunter enter the makeshift command center in the middle of nowhere, stopping in front of the table topped with the terrain model, which resembles the desert floor they flew over earlier.

"First, introductions are in order. This is Talbert H. W. Ambush."

The general points in the direction of a well-groomed, tall, slim official with intense eyes that complement his stone like facial features.

"And this is Mr. Hummel."

At first glance, the general favors Pin Head, from the movie Hell Raisers without the pins peppered all over his pale pasty like features. Instead, his face is accented by a pair of black framed military issued glasses. He, Mister Hummel is the supreme southern commanding officer of the secret military intelligence program Orange Spray.

Orange Spray is the ultra-secret intelligence-gathering unit for the army's Delta Force operatives. The Orange Spray program has operated under total anonymity for decades. All missions Delta Force operatives undertakes, are so secret that no one in the US government has access to the intelligence gathered by Orange Spray, except Talbert Ambush and a short list of other authorized government officials.

Finally, both Lieutenants Hunter and Slay are introduced to General Hopkins. Hopkins is the first black field grade officer to rise in the ranks in the special operation community, to become supreme commander of South America's JSOC forces. During his time in the ranks as a junior officer, he was teased by his superiors as being a spook in the flesh, or mister black ops, it was all done in fun.

The general oddly resembles the black superhero, Luke Cage, maybe that is why his tormentors made it clear to Hopkins that the name calling was done all in fun, to keep from being torn apart by the Ranger/Special Forces tab qualified officer. His reputation proceeds him, because of the success he achieves as the architect of the unsanctioned military operations in Nicaragua during the Reagan administration. Unfortunate, during this period in Nicaragua, a plane carrying a surplus of automatic weapons and other military munition was shot down, resulting in the capture of one of his men by Sandinista guerrillas. This compromise the mission and led to a US Senate Oversite investigation when the captive covert service member snitched that he was just following orders from his American commanding officer, who was never named in during the oversite investigation.

General Hopkins was also instrumental in the creation of the contra death squads, being financed by flooding major US cities with cocaine-smuggling operations out of Nicaragua by the CIA, when US Congress denies financial support for the military operations for South America JSOC forces.

General Hopkins was never held accountable, because he could never be linked in any way to the mess that exploded in Nicaragua.

Talbert H. W. Ambush is on site representing the National Security Agency, or, as Ambush likes to refer to his employer, No Such Agency. He will take control of the asset in question once Slay and Hunter recover it.

"I will be briefing you and Lieutenant Hunter about what you will be doing on this mission."

Ambush states.

"Let me just say you both are providing a great service for your country by taking on this task."

"This asset is vital to the national security of the United States," General Hopkins adds.

Lieutenant Hunter steps forward. "Sir, can I ask you a question?"

"Knock yourself out, Lieutenant."

Hunter displays his trademark smile. "Why us, sir? What made you choose me and Lieutenant Slay for this mission?"

General Hopkins steps forward to address Lieutenant Hunter's question. At the same time Ambush receives a weird vibe from someone in the makeshift command post, which rarely happens. Ambush is a hybrid human being, and only another hybrid human can give him such a vibe.

",I requested you two for this mission," Ambush announces, to Lieutenant Hunter's surprise. "I was in the situation room at JSOC during the assault at Noriega's compound and was impressed with the way you two handled that botched mission. After reading your military jackets, I requested your services."

In his research, Ambush discovered that both Rangers had been on a lot of covert operations in their short military careers, with a 100 percent completion rate to boot, though they had only been in the military two years. The special agent seized the moment to recruit fresh operatives for this black operations mission instead of recycled operatives who, in Ambush's opinion, tend to become complacent. Ambush can't afford complacency on this mission.

"You are both taking on a black ops asset-recovery mission."

Slay and Hunter glance in one another's direction.

"The asset that you two are to recover is a highly advanced device. If it were to fall into the wrong hands, it could pose a significant threat to US security and that of our allies."

"We believe the device is in this general area," General Hopkins says, indicating a location on the terrain map with a laser pointer.

ALIEN TECHNOLOGY

A mbush leans forward to give his input on the matter. "Gentlemen, this is what you are looking for."

He slides a picture of the device toward Slay and Hunter. The device is no bigger than an iPod and did not derive from this planet; it is alien technology. Ambush and the others have agreed not to reveal this information to Slay and Hunter, following (OPSEC) procedures. The window of opportunity is closing for the recovery of this alien technology, because foreign government agents are attempting to recover the alien technology for themselves. Orange Spray intel sources using unmanned drones have informed Mr. Hummel that the crash of the aircraft transporting the alien technology device wasn't accidental but rather a deliberate attack from a sophisticated surface-to-air missile system.

The perpetrators responsible for the attack have been identified as Russians.

The Soviet government has dispatched a Spetsnaz team to try to recover the asset before the Americans can do so. The upside to the situation is that the Russians don't have any idea what they are looking for; this will buy Slay and

Hunter a small window of opportunity to beat the Soviets to the punch.

Slay stares at Hunter, confirming that he's up for the challenge these ministers of death are offering them. Hunter affirms by displaying his trademark smile.

"Let me assure you, gentlemen, that we will be successful in recovering this device," Ronnie says.

"We have the utmost confidence in you both, or we wouldn't have chosen you for the mission. Let me assure you both that if either one of you makes the slightest mistake, the Russians won't hesitate to kill you, after torturing you for information.

"Take this time to study the picture of the device and burn it in your memory, because you won't be carrying anything that could assist the Russians in discovering the device."

Hunter feels a weird vibe he's never felt before; he dismisses it as fatigue. Hunter is unaware that he is a hybrid human as well and that the vibe he is receiving is coming from Talbert Ambush.

It's a scarlet night sky as the SBs zoom through the air. The copters are flying nap-of-the-earth to prevent being detected by radar or night vision equipment the Russians could be using. Slay and Hunter are inserted into a location not far from the recovery site without incident. They hastily take up a position on a hilltop, giving them an advantage against an enemy attack.

"Okay, Tony, game time. How're you feel?"

Lieutenant Hunter is busy setting up his sniper rifle. "I feel like we're being set up for slaughter, brah."

"Tony, I know the past couple of days have been real crazy, but this is how these guys work. They keep you in the dark—black ops, get it?"

"I get it, Ronnie. I don't have to like it, though. I want to know what the fuck I'm getting my ass into at all times."

Slay responds to his partner's bitch session with a grin. Then Slay takes out his binoculars to get a visual recon on the recovery site in the distance. It appears to be clear of any possible threats, as far as he can tell.

Before long Slay is set to head out to the recovery site. Ambush tells Ronnie to come back device so he and Hunter can get some well-deserved rest and relaxation.

Unknown to both Rangers, they are being shadowed by a four-man Spetsnaz team. The Russians are split into two-man teams; the first team is the counter-recon element. The others are the weapons element. They're responsible for shooting down the aircraft carrying the alien device when the word is given; they are to fire sixty-millimeter mortars on the hilltop to vaporize Lieutenant Hunter. The reconnaissance element will shadow Lieutenant Slay, watching his every move until he locates the device.

"Do you think this American will lead us to the device?" a Russian soldier asks.

"Comrade, I am sure this stupid American will lead us to the device. I am planning on it."

"Then we will take it after killing him, and I will give the order to weapons to blow his partner to bits," the leader of the team, Urkoroth, replies.

Lieutenant Slay arrives at the crash site. He thinks, *Shit,*

I was never good at Kim's Games.[30] I just hope I don't fuck up and fail to recognize this device. Lord, please help a brother out.

Lost in his thoughts, Slay is snapped back to reality by the desert's heat. This was one of Lieutenant Slay's weak points during Ranger School. He didn't care too much for the desert phase. The desert is an unforgiving place. Slay often thought of the desert as an alien environment that wasn't meant for human activity. Truth be told, Slay almost found himself being recycled[31] during the desert phase, because he failed to maintain the proper level of hydration and almost suffered a heat injury. But Slay is a hard charger; he dug deep inside and mustered the will to complete the demanding third phase of Ranger School; others have died trying to do so.

Even though Slay is still riding high on the fact he is involved on a black operation, negative thoughts keep creeping into his mind. He begins to think that maybe he and Tony are being used as pawns to draw out the Spetsnaz team.

In the back of his mind, Slay wonders if maybe it's the Russians who have the device. Maybe the plane really belongs to the Soviets, and the US is trying to steal this device from them. The aircraft bears no national symbols, known as a *sanitized aircraft*. But all that doesn't matter now, because Slay and Hunter are on the ground, totally committed to this secret mission to secure this device two powerful countries want very badly.

---

[30] Special operations training to develop a photographic memory.

[31] This term refers to the act of dropping trainees from Ranger School in hopes of them being picked up by another class.

After a while Slay comes across a huge depression he recognizes from the terrain model. He makes his way into the depression to begin his search. Slay conducts a radio check with Hunter, reporting his location and making sure Tony is safe and secure at his sniper position.

After searching most of the crash site, Lieutenant Slay has no luck finding the mysterious device. This makes the depression impact area his only hope of finding the asset. Just when he is about to throw his hands up in frustration, he spots what appears to be a combination briefcase partially buried in the sand inside a portion of the aircraft wreckage.

To Slay, this discovery is like finding a gold nugget in the middle of a rushing river. He also discovers the bodies of the pilots. Even though they are dressed in sanitized uniforms, their dog tags are of a NATO design, so he knows these men were Western Hemisphere service members. After securing the briefcase, Slay sits down inside the plane wreckage. The case is made of some type of hard plastic material, so all he should have to do is use some type of metal to crack the shell of the case.

PAWNS

Several minutes pass before Slay decides to use his M1 combat knife to crack the briefcase. The M1 combat knife features a thick, serrated, reinforced metal blade, pretty much unbreakable.

Slay stabs the case in the same general area over and over until the surface breaks. He begins sawing in the same area to make the hole bigger. Lieutenant Slay is able to put his hand inside the case, discovering a foam layer beneath the hard plastic shell. Carefully, he lifts the foam layer with his index and middle finger to feel some type of object. He cuts away more of the hard-plastic shell to expose the foam layer. He lifts it and observes an electronic device.

Meanwhile, Russian Spetsnaz approach just outside the aircraft wreckage.

Slay takes a closer look at the strange device, certain it is the asset he is to recover. He puts his weapon against the side of the aircraft wall, trying to find an on button or switch of some type.

Slay is startled by a noise from outside the wreckage. Before Slay can react, he finds himself in the presence of the enemy.

"We will take that, my American friend," Urkoroth says.

Before Slay can reach for his assault rifle, one of the Russians stops him, grabbing the weapon. Slay thinks, *I'm fucked. Why did I leave my weapon out of my fucking reach?*

The Russian soldier turns his attention back to Urkoroth. Slay takes advantage of this opportunity to quickly conceal his combat knife at the small of his back.

Urkoroth approaches Lieutenant Slay and takes the electronic device from him. "Thanks, my American friend. You have been of great service to Mother Russia." The Spetsnaz leader laughs out loud and marvels at the alien device, which he finds fascinating.

Slay looks for an opportunity to make his move to escape with the alien device and his life.

"Do you know why this device is so highly sought after, my American friend?"

Ronnie Slay doesn't say a word to the Russian; he just gives Urkoroth the thousand-yard stare.

"This device supposedly enables the user to travel either forward or backward in time, my American friend."

The Russian looks for a rise from Lieutenant Slay. When Urkoroth realizes that the American has no idea what he is talking about, he becomes amused. Slay is blown away by the Russian's comment but does his best to conceal his emotions.

Ronnie laughs out loud. "You've been drinking too much vodka, asshole."

"Ah, but it is true, my friend, and your insults will not change this truth. You were not aware that this device can do such a thing, no?"

Slay is vigilant to make his move to escape while making small talk with the Russians.

"I don't give a shit what you have to say, asshole. We all know you Russians are the biggest freakin' liars on the planet."

"Ah. Your superiors didn't tell you this important fact, no? Oh, I see. They just sent you out blind on this mission, because you are expendable in their eyes."

Ronnie thinks, *If this Russian prick is trying to get info from me, he's going about it in a weird fucking way.*

Slay dismisses the Russian's comment as bullshit. He can't be concerned with the Russian's babbling; he needs to make his escape with the asset.

The Russian holds up the device like a prize trophy as he continues to explain its value. He tells Slay that the Russian government will be able to go back into time to reverse historical events and straighten out the mess the Americans have created since becoming the modern superpower. Urkoroth says Russia will send time-travel operatives back into the past to reverse significant historical events that gave America its grip on power today, making Russia the undisputed superpower in the present and well into the future.

"Someone in your government has sold you a bill of goods, and played you for a fool."

You're full of shit. Traveling through time only happens in the movies. I don't believe you, jerk-off."

"What you believe is of no concern to me. You won't be around to see the new world we will create anyway, because you and your partner will be dead before we leave here today."

Slay is shocked that the Russian knows about Lieutenant Hunter.

"My partner will slit your guys' scalps from a thousand yards out before you can reach his position."

"Ah, but who said anything about approaching his position? You are familiar with crew-served weapons, such as mortars, yes? Once I give the command, your partner won't know what hit him."

Finally, Slay finds a window of opportunity. The second Russian takes his eyes off Slay to admire the lieutenant's modified AK-47 assault rifle. Before the Russian can return his attention to Slay, he finds himself choking on his own blood after Slay slams the blade of his combat knife into his throat. The dead Russian falls.

With catlike reflexes, Slay drops to the ground next to the dead Russian, grabs his assault rifle, and fires an automatic burst of full-metal-jacket rounds at the Spetsnaz leader, hitting him in his right shoulder area. The Russian twists violently to the ground, sending the time-travel device flying in the air. It lands close to Slay. Urkoroth makes a quick exit from the plane wreckage, clutching his right shoulder. Slay scrambles to his feet, locates the device, and places it in the cargo pocket of his pants.

Slay spots the Russian scrambling up the depression, using communication device as he does so. Slay realizes that the Russian is giving orders to fire on Hunter's position. Ronnie tries to contact Tony to warn him about the mortar attack.

"Sandman, this is Sandstorm—get out of there now! Displace! I say again, displace, Sandman!"

Lieutenant Hunter looks through his sniper scope to see if he can spot any movement around the depression, because he is getting concerned about not hearing from Lieutenant Slay.

The wind is blowing so hard Hunter can't hear the radio traffic coming from Slay.

"Ten-nine[32] your last, Sandstorm. Ten-nine," Lieutenant Hunter requests.

Lieutenant Hunter observes as the sky illuminates to his left front. Before the mortars impact his location, he sprints to his alternate position as fast as his legs will carry him. The mortars strike his primary position with a fire-for-effect result.

Back in the depression, after he hears the mortars explode in the distance, Slay thinks he has failed to save Hunter's life. He drops to one knee and fires his assault rifle at the fleeing Spetsnaz leader, hitting him in both legs, causing him to tumble back down into the depression.

---

[32] Communication code for "say again."

VENGEANCE BEST SERVED COLD

The Russian drops his radio after bullets strike both his legs. He tumbles to the bottom of the desert floor, screaming in pain. Urkoroth desperately tries to recover his radio but is prevented from doing so by Lieutenant Slay, who calmly walks over to the Russian and then kneels beside him.

"You killed a good friend of mine, you piece of shit, so here's what I'm going to do." Lieutenant pauses briefly to secure the Russians pistol.

"I will give you the device. After you have your men come to this location immediately."

The Russian struggles to sit up, a confused look on his face.

"You are asking me to lure my comrades to their deaths in exchange for the device, yes?"

"Give the man a cigar," Ronnie says in a sarcastic tone of voice. "Do we have a deal or not?"

"Yes, my American friend, we have a deal."

Ronnie hands the radio to the Spetsnaz leader, who in turn contacts his weapons team, instructing them to come to his location immediately. He tells them he has secured the device but has been wounded and needs medical aid quickly.

A flare illuminates the sky. Under Lieutenant Slay's watchful eye, Urkoroth returns fire with his flare gun, confirming his position to his men. Two huge Spetsnaz soldiers appear at the top of the depression. Not knowing whether the other American is dead or alive, they cautiously walk down the depression to provide aid to their leader.

"Comrade, did you kill the other American, or did he escape?"

The answer to the Russian's question is clear when Lieutenant Slay slowly walks from behind the plane wreckage, pointing his weapon at the startled Russians.

"No, he didn't kill me, scumbags."

They turn in the direction of Slays' voice, unable to engage him with their sidearms before Slay let's loose a burst of automatic fire at their feet. Both Russians drop their handguns to the ground and throw their hands straight up in the air. Ronnie keeps the muzzle of his weapon on the Russian soldiers.

"Move your sorry asses over there with your scumbag leader."

Without delay, both Russians move to where their leader is, a look of betrayal on their faces.

"Comrade Urkoroth, what is the meaning of this? Why is the American still alive? Why haven't you killed him?"

Urkoroth shrugs his shoulders.

"Because he has my pistol, you idiot. This is his plan—the American made me betray you both. For both your lives, he will give me the device our country wants so badly."

"That makes no sense, Comrade Urkoroth. Why?"

"For the advancement of the Motherland. You are not

more important than the mission, or have you forgotten our motto?"

"Motherland and mission above all."

Lieutenant Slay lines all the Russians up side by side, their leader at the end. He makes them interlock their fingers and instructs them to place their hands on top of their heads. Urkoroth scoots forward, away from his fellow countrymen, and struggles to stay on his feet.

"I have kept my word. Now keep yours."

Ronnie removes the alien device from his pants cargo pocket and tosses it to the wounded Russian.

Once Urkoroth has the device in his possession, Slay fires a burst of automatic fire at the other two Spetsnaz soldiers, killing them both instantly. Urkoroth is the last Russian left standing in front of Lieutenant Slay.

The Spetsnaz leader is physically shaken after watching Slay execute his men in such a brutal manner. The Russian doesn't dare let the crazy American know he has just pissed his pants out of fear. Slowly Urkoroth wipes away blood and brain matter from his face.

"It is a shame that they had to be sacrificed for the mission, but they will be honored as heroes back in Mother Russia. I will see to this, my fallen comrades," Urkoroth says in a low voice.

Slay feels nothing but contempt for Urkoroth. He points his weapon in the Russian's direction.

"You really are a fucking lowlife scumbag, aren't you?" Slay says in a stern tone of voice.

"What is the meaning of this? You said we had a deal. I lure my men to their death, and you let me go with the device. You are big liar!" The Russian says in extreme rage. Slay gives Urkoroth the look of death before responding.

"I kept my end of the deal. I gave you the device. I never said you would leave here with it alive." Slay chuckles before continuing.

"You told me earlier that I won't be around to see the new world order."

"Well, it looks like you're the one who won't be around to see the *novus ordo seclorum*, shit for brains."

Lieutenant Slay tosses Urkoroth's pistol back at him; it lands next to his feet. The Russian looks down at his handgun and succeeds in picking it up.

Slay releases his assault rifle grip, letting the weapon dangle from its sling as he draws his Desert Eagle handgun. He fires two well-placed rounds into the Russian's forehead.

Urkoroth never knew what hit him; he is dead before hitting the ground. The wind begins to blow hard around Lieutenant Slay as he approaches the dead Russian.

"That's for Tony, motherfucker."

Slowly Slay returns his handgun to its holster and stands over the Russian corpse, admiring his marksmanship. He hit the Russian in the band of death, or the middle of the forehead, blowing off a third of the Russian's skull with the hydro shock rounds. When bullets strike the brain in such a lethal way, the body's muscle functions lock up, causing the person to place a death grip on whatever might be in his or her possession—in this case, the alien device. Without hesitation Slay pries open the dead Russian's hand and retrieves the alien device.

Lieutenant Slay then heads back to the dark site in an SB. He asks the pilot to take him to the hilltop position so he can check on Lieutenant Hunter, in hopes of recovering his friend's corpse. The copter touches down on the hilltop. The destruction to Lieutenant Hunter's sniper position is enormous. Slay leaps out of the copter, hoping to at least recover his best friend's dog tags.

A voice calls, "Hey, hotshot, what took you so long?"

Slay spots Lieutenant Hunter walking toward him with that trademark smile on his face.

"What the fuck, you're alive!" Slay bursts into uncontrolled laughter. "How in the hell did you manage to escape the mortar attack?"

"A good sniper always has a backup plan. When I saw the flash of mortar fire, I displaced to my alternate position, and I prayed like never before."

Ronnie grabs Tony around the waist and lifts him off his feet. Both soldiers laugh out loud.

"If you didn't come out here to check on me, I would have never forgiven you, Ronnie."

"That's the least I could do for you, Tony."

"Our creed: no Ranger gets left behind."

They load into the helicopter, and shortly, the SB touches down on the helipad of the dark site. Slay exits the copter, followed by Lieutenant Hunter. They slowly walk to the command center tent and enter.

"Welcome back, Lieutenant Slay, Hunter. We heard you both had close calls. Let me be the first to congratulate you both on avoiding being killed," General Hopkins says. "In any event, I trust you have recovered the classified asset?"

Ronnie Slay reaches very slowly into his pants cargo pocket to remove the device and then slams it on the table in front of General Hopkins. "There's your precious fucking device! I almost lost a good friend recovering your garbage!"

General Hopkins turns in the direction of Talbert Ambush, shock on his face over Lieutenant Slays' behavior.

Ambush calmly walks over to the table to retrieve the device; he doesn't appear to be upset by Lieutenant Slays' behavior. The special agent knows it is impossible for Lieutenant Slay, or anything else, to damage the alien device, since it's not made of any indigenous material from planet Earth.

General Hopkins approaches Lieutenant Slay and gets in his face. "Your behavior has gotten your ass in a shit sandwich you're not going to like eating, Lieutenant! I will personally see to it that you receive a dishonorable discharge, as well as a court-martial for behavior unbecoming to a commissioned officer! When I'm done, you won't be able to get a job as a janitor!"

Ambush secures the device on his person before intervening in the heated situation between Lieutenant Slay and General Hopkins.

Uncle Bush Wants You

Lieutenant Slay laughs out loud; he isn't intimidated by General Hopkins's threats.

"I don't give a damn about what suits' can do to me; we just fought off Russian special forces troops who knew our location. Basically, me and Hunter were used as pawns for your fucking quest to recover that so-called time-travel device!"

General Hopkins's and Hummel's eyes widen when Slay refers to the mysterious electronic piece of equipment as a time-travel device.

"Who the hell told you that?" General Hopkins asks. He walks up to Lieutenant Slay with rage and indignation on his face. The silence in the command center can be cut with a knife.

Ambush walks over to the upset government official and nudges General Hopkins away from Lieutenant Slay.

"There won't be any fucking court-martial hearing or dishonorable discharges happening to anyone today or any other time, especially to these American heroes. Besides, how can you court-martial them on issues connected to a black operations mission that doesn't exist?

"Not to mention the issue that doing so would result in media exposure about Russian soldiers operating in a Western Hemisphere combat zone controlled by US forces. We all would be made a laughingstock in the military community, not to mention being banned from ever serving in the government again and possibly being committed to a mental institution."

Talbert Ambush basically acknowledges that Lieutenant Slay has a right to be upset; he and Hunter were both used as pawns by a shadow government that doesn't exist as far as the public is concerned. This isn't exactly how Slay imaged things on his first black operation would turn out. There has been too much secrecy, backroom planning, and gambling with the lives of brave warriors, discarding them like garbage. But all the courage and can-do attitude executed by the elite men and women who operate in the shadows will never be known by the American people they serve and die for. Black operatives are the unknown soldiers, the quiet professionals who will never be acknowledged by the government, because their missions are top secret in nature, as is the case for Lieutenant Slay and Hunter.

But Talbert Ambush confirms and acknowledges to Slay and Hunter that, indeed, the device is capable of time travel. That's the least he can do for the two of them for putting their lives on the line for their country.

Hopkins and Hummel can't believe Ambush would talk openly about top secret information with individuals who are not authorized to know national security information.

"With this device we will maintain power around the world, which is constantly in danger of being threatened by forces seeking to inflict genocide on masses of people they see as inferior.

"Here's my card. Give me a call if either one of you should tire of playing GI Joe and want to venture deeper into the black operations community on a regular basis. If you call, ask to speak with Uncle Bush."

Ambush nods, silently giving Hopkins and Hummel a heads-up that he is ready to leave Panama. He returns his attention to Lieutenants Slay and Hunter.

"By the way, Noriega was apprehended by US forces as he attempted to hide in a church in Panama City. Again, outstanding job to you both on that reconnaissance mission. I thought you both should know your efforts helped bring about his capture."

All three high-level government officials board one of the quiet birds, leaving the temporary site as if they were never there.

Slay looks at Hunter. "Uncle Bush. That guy is fucking weird and a freaking fluke if you ask me," Slay says in a low tone of voice.

Hunter's trademark smile crosses his face. "Must be Uncle Sam's evil twin, brah."

They both laugh out loud in the middle of nowhere.

ONE AND DONE

The days in Panama fade away as Captain Slay wakes up from his nap.

It's 1991; Iraq had the third-largest army in the world has invaded the small country of Kuwait, ordered there by a renegade Iraqi dictator menace. The American public is convinced by the media that the Iraqi leader is taking advantage of the small country of Kuwait. In fact, government officials aligned with the Shadow Government Oversight Panel of Thirteen (SGOPT) are using the situation to send representatives from US oil companies to Kuwait on a false-flag operation.[33] This is done to create the climate for the United States to gain a presence in the Middle East to establish a forward military base of operations.

National Security Council officials connected with the SGOPT have instructed these oil-company representatives to drill under Kuwaiti soil into Iraq, in order to steal Iraqi oil.

This unsanctioned operation will kill several political birds with one covert operational stone to achieve the

---

[33] Unsanctioned covert operations designed to cause the appearance of enemy sovereignties abusing their power.

following: the United States will get oil without paying for it and provoke the Iraqi dictator into attacking Kuwait, the US government will gain public support for an invasion of Iraq, America will gain a presence in the Middle East, and OPEC will corner the global oil market.

Essentially, this false-flag operation will clear the way for an invasion into Iraq and will allow the United States to seize their oil supply.

The United States is targeting Iraq because Iraq purposely increased their oil prices to make it difficult for America to afford an operational supply of oil for the US military. The current sitting Iraqi leader has been a thorn in the side of the US government for decades.

The Iraqis refuse to negotiate a fair price for their oil, which they have every right to do. But this causes a price war on a global scale with one of America's closest allies, OPEC, which is extremely outraged about this global dilemma. The Saudis must raise the price of their oil as well. Gas prices will also rise for the American public.

The Chinese are laughing all the way to the bank, because they are getting their oil supply at wholesale prices from Nigeria. This price war places the United States in a bad situation, because America has an agreement to buy their oil exclusively from Saudi Arabia for the next decade. Because of Iraq's reckless behavior, the Saudis demand that the United States place economic sanctions on Iraq.

Meanwhile the Chinese are taking advantage of the international unrest to build up their military machine in their quest to challenge America's global superpower status. Intelligence sources have reported that the Iraqi leadership apparatus is destabilizing the global oil markets purposely, in an effort to help the Chinese reach global dominance over the United States and its allies. This outcome will benefit the Iraqis as well, because, in return, China has pledged to make Iraq one of its closest allies in every way.

This partnership will destabilize the Middle East in the worst way, because the Iraqis are known adversaries of Israel. With the Chinese government backing the renegade Iraqi dictator, nothing will stop him from attacking Israel with his weapons of mass destruction. Should the United States become engaged in a world war with China? The Chinese will have no trouble waging a global war against America. They have more than enough military resources to wage war overseas and simultaneously defend their mainland.

This isn't the case for America; its military is already stretched thin by budget reductions and cutbacks. A full-scale war with China will leave Israel vulnerable to an attack by Iraq.

SGOPT officials have sent oil-company representatives to Kuwait as a Trojan horse to infiltrate the region undetected. Again, these company representatives have been instructed to steal oil from Iraq and provoke Iraq to attack the Kuwaitis, giving the United States a window of opportunity to gain the presence in the Middle East it so badly wants. The false-flag operation is a major success. Not only does the United States get crude oil for nothing, the US government also gets the support of the American people for the invasion into Iraq. But most importantly, the United States gets the opportunity to get rid of the current pain-in-the-ass Iraqi leadership once and for all.

At an operational briefing at Hunter Army Airfield,

in Savannah, Georgia, Captains Slay and Hunter go over footnotes as they listen in.

You wouldn't know that you were on a military installation, because the briefing hall looks more like a college facility. The only difference between this lecture-style auditorium and a college structure is that instead of academic icons, military icons line the walls.

The auditorium is filled with leadership personnel from the First Ranger Battalion. A major specializing in operational intel is briefing the group. He is in awesome shape, with the facial features of a man who has seen his share of combat missions.

Every seat in the auditorium is filled with high-level commissioned and noncommissioned officers who will receive information on what their units will be doing in the invasion into Iraq. The conference auditorium has the smell of musk and bug spray. The invasion of Iraq will commence at 0200 hours, Zulu time.[34]

First Ranger Battalion long-range reconnaissance p atrol (LRRP) scout snipers will deploy ahead of the assault element. Captain Slay is the commanding officer; Captain Hunter is second in command. The LRRP mission is to eliminate high-ranking Iraqi officials in order to destabilize the Iraqi government.

Photographs of all known heads of state in Iraq are currently being passed around so the scouts can familiarize themselves with their targets. Rules of engagement: terminate with extreme prejudice.

This action comes as a response to Iraq's invasion of

---

[34] UTC.

Kuwait. The US president has activated the rapid-deployment force to come to the defense of Kuwait, because this small nation has no standing army to defend its sovereignty. It is considered a close ally. Intelligence reports confirm this attack against Kuwait is unprovoked on the Kuwaitis' part.

It is believed the Iraqi military is committing genocide against the people of Kuwait in an effort to seize that country's oil supply, an international crime perpetrated by the Iraqi leadership and military—not to mention a national security threat to the United States and its allies.

"Any questions, gentlemen?"

Captain Slay raises his hand. "Sir, we are to eliminate all high-ranking Iraqi officials, correct?"

"That's correct, Captain."

Slay rubs his forehead.

"Sir, wouldn't it be beneficial to capture these dirt bags to gather any intelligence they can provide us about what the Iraqis are up to?"

The auditorium erupts with laughter.

"All right, quiet down. Negative, Captain. This is a covert op, not a fact-finding mission! We don't base our actions on hypotheticals; we follow orders. I say again, the country of Iraq has overstepped its boundaries and must be stopped at all costs. Is that clear, Captain?"

Slay nods very slowly. "Clear, sir."

The field grade officer stares Captain Slay down from his position on the auditorium stage. To the officer's amazement, Slay returns the stare-down tactic. The major concludes that the young captain isn't the least bit intimidated by him. In fact, Slay appears to be looking straight through the staff officer. The major has seen this type of behavior before from soldiers who have had a brush with death in the bush more than once and who consider death as an ally, not something to fear.

The mission brief is complete. Captain Slay, Captain Hunter, and the rest of the scouts are flown to Pope Air Force Base for deployment, spearheading the Iraq invasion.

High in the sky inside a sanitized aircraft, Slay and Hunter discuss the mission through audio headsets.

"Hey, Ronnie, what do you think about this mission?"

Slay looks up from the mug shots of the Iraqi officials he and his team are to terminate during their mission. "I think we're being sent on a fucking assassination mission sanctioned by our government."

Captain Hunter leans his forehand against the barrel of his sniper rifle. "Is that a bad thing, brah?"

"It is to me, Tony. As a nation, we need to set the example for the rest of the world as a moral country."

"I disagree. We're talking about Iraq, a country that gasses women and children to death. For what? Because they want a better way of life for themselves and their families."

An individual approach Slay and Hunter from their left flank to eavesdrop on their conversation through his own audio headset. This mysterious figure turns out to be none other than Special Agent Ambush, the governmental official who oversaw their black operations mission in Panama years before.

"Gentlemen, mind if I join your conversation?"

Slay and Hunter are taken by surprise by Agent Ambush's sudden presence. Slay immediately recognizes Talbert Ambush. Hunter rises to his feet and greets the special agent with a handshake.

"What are you doing here, sir?"

Agent Ambush shakes Captain Hunter's hand and experiences a strange vibration that puzzles him. But he has other matters to tend to now.

"I'm in charge of this mission, Captain Hunter."

Ambush isn't the least bit surprised to notice Slay and Hunter have both been promoted to the rank of captain; he was instrumental in having them fast-tracked to their current rank.

"Good to see you again, Captain Slay. Congratulations to you both on your promotions."

Ronnie reluctantly extends his hand toward the special agent.

"Did I hear you telling Hunter you're in charge of this mission?" Slay asks.

"That's correct, Captain. I'm going to play in the sandbox with you both and get my hands dirty."

Ambush wears a tight grin that reminds Slay of the cat that swallowed the canary.

"So, you're fine leading an assassination mission?" Slay returns Ambush's tight grin.

Ambush raises his eyebrows.

"Please, I told you the last time we saw one another to call me Uncle Bush."

Slay smirks.

"You do realize Captain Slay, that our government doesn't condone assassination of any kind?"

"This is an HVN[35] operation targeting heads of state who run an out-of-control rogue government with WMDs that has invaded an ally of ours, that's all."

---

[35] High-value neutralization.

Hunter sits back down in his seat, looking at Slay as if he has just won the lottery.

"See, brah, we're still the good guys after all."

"This is a covert operation, nothing more, nothing less," Ambush replies.

Slay doesn't believe Agent Ambush. After all, Ambush works for one of the most secretive intelligence agencies in the world and knows how to spin a lie to sound like the truth.

Slay turns his attention back to Hunter. And says;

"Brah, believe nothing that you're told and only half of what you see. This guy makes a living from smoke and mirrors and slick talk."

Captain Slay tells Ambush he believes the officials targeted for death could be sources of intelligence to assist the American combat forces in fighting and ultimately defeating the Iraqi Army.

Agent Ambush reaches out and takes all the mug shots Slay is still holding. He sorts through most of them and returns all but one to Slay.

Ambush displays the photo. Then he explains that the person in the photo, wearing a military uniform and a black beret, who attended and graduated from the Division Leadership War College at Fort Leavenworth, Kansas, was the architect behind the mustard gas incident on the Kurds several years ago. Masses of innocent people were slaughtered, mostly women and children. The atrocity happened because this psychopath, who goes by the name of Dr. Propaganda, has the backing and support of the Iraqi leadership to do whatever he pleases. Agent Ambush tells Slay and Hunter it is imperative that Dr. Propaganda is neutralized at all costs. If they don't neutralize Dr. Propaganda, he will not hesitate to use chemical agents against American forces and allies.

Slay looks toward Hunter. "Like hell he will—not if we can help it."

Agent Ambush hands the photo back to Slay. The flight chief instructs Agent Ambush to prep his detail for their HALO jump into the Iraqi desert.

High in the Iraqi night sky, ministers of death, along with Agent Ambush, silently descend to the earth. The commandos and Ambush scramble for cover in a trench that skirts the road near their landing location. There, the soldiers and Ambush discard their parachute gear.

Captain Slay directs his scouts to set up inboard and outboard security over watch positions.

Slay and Hunter go over the map of Baghdad, rechecking grid coordinates one last time before moving out. One of Slay's scouts tells him vehicles can be heard in the distance.

Everybody lies down in the trench to wait out the convoy traffic. The Iraqi desert is silent once again. Slay and Hunter are informed the mechanized convoy was made up of troop transport vehicles escorted by light armored attack vehicles, heading in the direction of the city of Baghdad.

Slay signals for all the scouts to gather around to receive final instructions about their mission. All the commandos ensure that their weapons and gear are properly prepped before heading out to hunt down and kill unsuspecting Iraqi officials.

Should time allow, the commandos are to terminate secondary targets—corrupt law enforcement officials as well as militiamen. Per protocol, the commandos memorize their targets; they will not carry any intel on their persons, to avoid compromising their missions. All the physical intel material is incinerated in place with dissolving liquid.

"At all costs, your primary targets must be eliminated," Ambush reminds the two-man assassin teams.

The commandos' success is vital to clear the way for the assault force's invasion of Baghdad. Captain Hunter gives every commando egress codes about their extraction points, plus alternate egress points out of Baghdad.

The scouts head into the desert under the cover of darkness. Slay, Hunter, and Agent Ambush remain in place. Ambush double-checks his small patrol pack to ensure all his equipment is accounted for. He is most concerned with ensuring he can account for the T-3D, the time-travel-technology device. No bigger than an iPod, it's easy to lose track of.

US intelligence has discovered the Russians have aligned themselves with China, N Korea, Cuba, calling this the 'Eastern Alliance' and to the US that also have time-travel technology capabilities.

Talbert H. W. Ambush thinks, *The race is on to prevent our nemesis from attacking our past, our present, and, most of all, our children's future.*

Hunter wears his trademark smile as he nudges Slay. "Hey, brah, watch this."

Hunter whispers to the special agent, "Hey, Uncle Bush, we're ready to move out. Think you'll be able to keep up with us?"

Ambush secures the T-3D in its carrier.

"Of course, I can. My pack weighs all of twenty pounds. You tough guys are the ones carrying the mother lode, so lead the way."

BACK TO THE FUTURE

After several hours of patrolling, the three men halt to hydrate themselves. Even at night, the desert can rapidly sap fluids from a person's body. Ambush takes this opportunity to make a communications check with JSOC and update command with intel on the motorized convoy they encountered earlier.

Command informs Ambush that Dr. Propaganda is overseeing command of all Iraqi forces, working out of the royal palace in Baghdad. The intelligence confirms that Doctor Propaganda orders half of the Iraqi Army back to Baghdad.

Ambush makes sure to catch both Slay and Hunter up on the current intel from JSOC. He also ensures both commandos know they have less than eight hours before US forces arrive in country, so time is of the essence. They must get to the target area ASAP.

The three operators reach the outskirts of Baghdad. Ambush uses binoculars to scout the area. Predawn is approaching, so swiftness is of the utmost importance to secure the objective area of operations (OAO) and avoid compromising the mission. There is little to no activity on the streets. The operatives take advantage of the situation, quickly moving to the back of a warehouse.

"Heads up, troops—it's showtime. See that big fancy building at one o'clock?" Ambush asks.

Slay and Hunter give him thumbs-up signals, confirming they see the reference point.

"That's where Dr. Propaganda is overseeing military operations of the Iraqi military. On top of that building, at eleven o'clock, is where the shooting position is to be set up."

Captain Slay turns his attention to Agent Ambush. "And how do you suppose we do that? We'll stick out like a sore thumb as soon as we hit the streets."

Ambush quickly checks his watch. "If you haven't yet noticed, this is a supply warehouse, full of all types of uniforms we can use to disguise our appearance."

Hunter is displays his trademark smile.

"The KISS method. I like it, Uncle Bush."

He gives Slay a fist pound, and the three men enter the supply warehouse. Once inside, they begin searching for utility uniforms to disguise themselves. Each man secures a uniform that fits loosely to conceal sidearm bulges. They also find equipment bags to store their military gear and primary weapons in. All three operatives exit the warehouse on their way toward the high-rise building.

Ambush tells Slay and Hunter to remain quiet should they encounter any authorities. He lets them know he is fluent in several Arabic dialects and will address any issues that might arise.

There is very little activity on the streets. The citizens have been told to stay indoors for safety from the inevitable

American invasion. Despite the warnings, some Iraqi citizens are heading out of Baghdad, attempting to flee the city before the bullets start to fly. Business owners attempt to salvage their supplies to avoid them being destroyed by military forces when battle erupts in their streets.

The three men gain access to the high-rise without incident. It's eerie inside; the hallways resemble a ghost town. Most of the apartment doors are wide open, exposing tenants' property for thieves to loot. One apartment gets all three operatives' attention, as an American flag has been used as a doormat.

Ambush seems unfazed. That is far from the truth. He's simply been in the game long enough to keep his emotions in check and is a constant professional, remaining focused on the mission at hand.

Before long, Ambush leads Slay and Hunter to the top floor, coming to a stop in front of the rooftop door. Written on it in Arabic are the words *generator room*. Ambush tells Slay and Hunter they will find a giant air-conditioning unit; this is where they are to construct the shooting position.

Hunter whispers to Slay in a sarcastic manner, "I like the way Uncle Bush says we can set up the shooting position."

Ambush turns the doorknob to the generator room gently. "Did you say something, Captain Hunter?"

Hunter, realizing Ambush overheard his comment, clears his throat. "Uh, naw, Uncle Bush."

Ambush tells Hunter to clear his mind and focus on the task at hand, because after they pass through the door, there will be no mistakes allowed.

They enter the generator room; Ambush proceeds to shut off all power to the building. Slay and Hunter head out to the roof to set up their sniper site. Ambush places motion-detector explosives on the inside of the generator door, to prevent an attack from the enemy. Then he contacts command to check in. He is told that stealth bombers are now on standby to provide surgical air support for his mission to assassinate Sheikh Khalid, Dr. Propaganda's given name. Ambush is directed to laser the palace when the sniper team takes their shot, synchronizing the bomb strike to hit at the same time, thus ensuring complete annihilation of Dr. Propaganda and the goons protecting him.

A motorcade arrives at the gate of the royal palace. Ambush joins Slay and Hunter at the sniper site. The positions is well hidden by the huge reinforced steel air-conditioning units. Slay and Hunter set up urban camouflage nets to conceal their location from being detected from above, along with foam mats for relief from the hard concrete floor, to ensure the most accurate shot possible can be fired downrange.

Ambush slowly goes to one knee, using binoculars to observe the activity below.

"Listen up, troops. Command has informed me that the invasion of Iraq is about to kick off."

Ambush removes a unit challenge coin from his utility pants pocket, gives it a kiss, and holds it up to the sky before he returns it to his pants pocket. Neither Slay nor Hunter are disturbed by the federal agent's actions; both Rangers have seen other warriors in the special ops community perform this same behavior before engaging the enemy in armed combat.

"Looks like the god of war is smiling down on us today, troops. Let's send him some souls to judge."

Shortly, several military vehicles carrying troops pull up at the palace to provide reinforcement for the Republican Guard. Ambush assembles a sophisticated eavesdropping device designed for voice detection. All Ambush has to do is aim it toward a desired location to pick up voice patterns, providing the sniper team with the precise location of their target. Unknown to Slay and Hunter, this electronic also doubles as a missile laser guidance system. Ambush will use it to guide in smart bombs as overkill insurance to ensure Sheikh Khalid is vaporized.

Ambush confirms the location of their target. Small arms fire and explosions are audible in the far distance.

The data confirms the target is on the thirteenth floor.

"Okay, gents, we're on. I've located our target on the thirteenth floor, outboard side. Do you confirm the same?"

Slay, the spotter, confirms the visual data with Ambush. As directed by command, Ambush transmits the data to the pilots. They await his signal to launch their deadly payload. Agent Ambush lights up the middle of the building with his laser sight, invisible to the naked eye. Then he gives the sniper team the command to go hot. Hunter makes final sight adjustments.

Simultaneously, Ambush gives the pilots the go signals to go hot. They fire their missiles and then head back to their base of operations.

Hunter exhales, confirming his target in his scope's crosshairs, and squeezes the trigger of his weapon. A full-metal-jacket round shatters Sheikh Khalid's skull. His brain spatters on the opposite wall in the room. Instant chaos and panic erupt from the occupants in the room.

Missiles slam into the building simultaneously with

deadly efficiency. Every window of the high-rise is blown out on the side where the sniper position is.

The air-conditioning apparatus protects all three operatives from being shredded to death by the fallout of glass raining down on their position. Once all the glass stops falling, Slay, Hunter, and Ambush check themselves to ensure they are in one piece; they rise, coughing and wiping off residue from their uniforms.

Slay erupts with extreme rage. He approaches Ambush. "What the fuck was that!"

Ambush remains calm and continues to wipe dust residue from his uniform. As Slay closes the distance, he checks his electronics for accountability.

Slay violently grabs Ambush around his neck. Ambush responds by shoving his sidearm directly in Slay's gut.

"You're out of line, Captain. I suggest you compose yourself. I have no qualms about firing a bullet point-blank into your gut. Let go of my neck."

Slay releases his grip and steps back, away from the muzzle of Ambush's handgun.

"What the fuck was that? You almost killed us all with your cowboy tactics!"

Hunter walks over, pulling Slay away from Ambush. "Ronnie, chill out. Compose yourself, brah. Don't do anything you'll regret later."

Slay calms down a little. "That crazy bastard killed innocent people on the streets, and he doesn't seem to give a fuck."

Ambush secures his gear as artillery explodes in the distance. "Look around you, Captain! There's a war erupting around us, and in war people die. There are no innocents, only volunteers. Stop walking around with your eyes shut. They need to be open wide."

"Open wide to what?"

"To how power is maintained, Captain Slay!"

"How is power maintained? By killing civilians, Uncle Bush?"

Ambush reaches into the left breast pocket of his battle dress top and removes the T-3D.

GIVE ME LIBERTY, OR
GIVE ME DEATH

"Recognize this, huh?"

Slay and Hunter immediately recognize the alien device they recovered for Ambush a couple of years ago.

"That's the device me and Hunter recovered for you in Panama back in '89."

"Bingo! That's right."

"What the hell does that have to do with anything?"

Ambush explains to both men that today's events have been brought on by the Eastern Alliance, using the same T-3D technology. According to Orange Spray intelligence reports, Eastern Alliance has sent time travel agent back into time to alter historic events to erode America's grip on global power and to take control of that power for themselves.

Slay and Hunter burst out in laughter over Ambush's explanation. Hunter waves him off as he heads back to the sniper position. Slay stays put and thinks, *I always felt these cloak-and-dagger guys were a little off. But now I'm convinced they're just plain insane.*

At first, Ambush can't decide whether to be disappointed by Slays' and Hunter's attitudes or to just shoot them dead and let God sort it out. He decides to show Slay how important the T-3D is to their country. Ambush reminds him about the proposition he made to both him and Hunter in Panama in 1989. Slay reluctantly acknowledges that he remembers the conversation.

Ambush tells Slay,

"If I can prove the T-3D is vital to national security, I want you to resign from the military and join the NSA." Captain Slay just agrees, because he doesn't believe anything coming out the mouth Ambush.

"All right,"

"But if you fail to do so, I want you to turn yourself in to the chain of command to face charges for war crimes." Ambush just grins and nods his head in agreement.

And then, Ambush explains to Slay that Orange Spray Intelligence has uncovered a plot in which the Eastern Alliance[36] recently sent a time-travel agent back in time which brought about today's events in an effort to seize global power from the United States. Ambush also tells the young captain that he will take him back into time to bear witness to how the reversal of things past can be weaponized to alter the future in a negative or positive way.

Both men shake hands in agreement to prove the other wrong.

Command informs Ambush that a marine division will be rolling into Baghdad, and needs suppression support, sniper fire in layman terms. Hunter, being a sniper is tasked with providing sniper support for the Marines.

---

[36] An alliance consisting of Russia, China, Nigeria, North Korea, Iraq, and Nicaragua.

For some reason, Ronnie Slay feels like he is abandoning Tony Hunter, but Captain Slay feels strongly sense of duty to prove Ambush a liar about having the ability to travel into time. Captain Slay has confidence Hunter will be able to handle himself alone under pressure in a war zone.

Hunter is excited about the prospect of operating on his own, especially providing sniper support for a marine division. He has the utmost admiration and respect for marines. Hunter views Devil Dogs[37] as an extension of the elite creed—brother warriors.

Ambush ensures that Hunter has the remote control to the explosives attached to the rooftop door, as well as the call signs to the marine division commanders.

Ambush tells Slay he won't need anything other than his uniform for the trip into the past; it would alter time if he were to lose anything from the future in the past. So, Slay leaves everything but his uniform with Hunter and gives his regards to him, telling him he'll be right back. Slay tells Hunter he's only humoring Uncle Bush about this time-travel garbage.

Slay returns to Ambush's location. The special agent removes the T-3D and punches in a date and time on its digital screen. He initiates the activation button. A bright light in the shape of a door appears. Slay raises his arm to shield his eyes from the brightness. Ambush enters the bright light, followed by Slay. Hunter stares in disbelief. Just as quickly as the light appeared, it's gone in the twinkle of an eye.

"What the fuck, Ronnie? What have you gotten yourself into, brah?"

---

[37] Nickname the Germans gave American marines during WWI.

SECRET WAR FOR GLOBAL POWER

Slay finds himself speeding through time. He feels like he's in a dream state. As he turns his head to his immediate left, he observes a ball of light; instinctively he figures it's Talbert H. W. Ambush. Slay looks to his front to observe sprinkles of light zooming past him at the speed of light.

His body becomes consumed by comfortable warmth, and his consciousness is filled with unexplainable peace. Without his knowledge, Slay's clothing is transformed to match the time era he and Ambush are heading to. Ronnie is now experiencing the phenom known as nirvana.

The feeling comes to an end as the bright light in the shape of a door opens again. Ambush exits into the past, followed by Slay. As soon as Slay clears the time porthole, the door of light disappears in the twinkle of an eye. Had there been anyone in the immediate area of the time porthole, they would have been frozen in place due to the manipulation of time that the vortex vacuum created when the door of light opened.

Slay is stunned to realize that they are no longer on the rooftop in Iraq anymore. Both Ambush and Slay are now in Switzerland. He stumbles around in the open while Ambush secures a couple of identification credentials in a conference room next door. Ambush knows they will need the credentials to gain access to the G-6 Summit, a secret meeting where allied rogue nations come together to discuss important policy issues they wish to impose throughout the world.

The *G* represents the word *global*, and the number 6 represents the six nations in attendance to discuss the world events on their itinerary. The list of nations represented are China, Soviet Union, North Korea, Iraq, Nicaragua, and Nigeria.

Slays' mind is slowly emerging from a mental fog. He peeks inside a conference room and spots Ambush moving about, gathering what he needs for their cover.

"There you are, Ronnie my boy. Still have doubts about time travel? Trust me—I know how you feel. My first time was mind-blowing too. Right now, we have to move fast if we want to keep from being discovered by the authorities."

"Where are we? We never left Baghdad, did we? This is one of your agency's psychological tricks, right?"

"Look around you—does this look like a freakin' trick? We're in Switzerland in 1988, where the plan to destabilize the Middle East was hatched. Now, what I need you to do is clear your fucking head, if you want to return to the future in one piece."

Ambush hands Slay an ID for an Iraq man, the government official he will masquerade as at the summit. Ambush assures Slay he will soon explain everything, but, now, they have more important things to attend to, like verifying the room number where their targets are.

Slay walks around in the conference room, looking at documents lying out in the open on a table. He picks up a Swiss newspaper, which happens to be dated 1988. The headlines: "Libyan Terrorist Bomb Explodes on Pan Am Jet over Lockerbie."

Ambush finds a Swiss security roster with the room number of their targets.

"Our targets are located on the fourth floor. Let's go."

He and Slay make their way to the fourth floor after making a quick stop at the medical office to secure sedatives Ambush plans to use on the dignitaries to render them unconscious.

Dressed in waiter attire, they take the elevator to the designated floor. Before knocking on the door, Ambush gives Slay last-minute instruction on what to do once they are in the room with the Iraqi officials.

Ambush knocks on the door; a middle-aged man opens the door.

"Can I help you?"

"I apologize for disturbing you. We're here to take your order for breakfast, sir. May we come in?"

The man appears confused but allows them in. They stop in the middle of the hotel suite. Suddenly, Ambush is on top of the Iraqi, sticking him with a hypodermic needle and quickly rendering the man unconscious. Ambush places the man on the couch and gives Slay hand and arm signals to look for the second Iraqi. Slay finds him asleep in the adjacent bedroom, being very careful as to not to wake the Iraqi Diplomat.

Slay quickly removes the safety cap on his syringe and

sticks the Iraqi. The man's eyes open but quickly close as he becomes unconscious.

Ambush enters the bedroom. "Okay, we need to hurry before the summit begins. Check the closet for a suit to change into."

Ambush goes to the other bedroom to grab a suit for himself. They find what they need. As Slay comes out of the room, he is shocked, ready to come to blows with a man he believes is another Iraqi man. The crazy thing about the situation is this Iraqi man looks identical to the Iraqi who answered the door earlier.

"What the fuck!"

Ronnie picks up the nearest object to strike the Iraqi.

"Hold on! It's me, Uncle Bush! I've assumed the identity of our friend on the couch."

Slay glances over at the couch, and there, still unconscious, is the actual Iraqi dignitary.

"We just have to exchange the other guy's facial features with yours. Hand over the ID I gave you earlier." Ambush removes his T-3D and then proceeds to take a picture of Slay. This procedure saves Slay's facial features in the device's memory bank.

This process is called facial-cloning analysis; this technology is cousin to the hologram and is known as a solid gram mask. It gives operatives the ability to assume the appearance, voice pattern, and mannerisms of the subject they are disguised as.

Both Ambush and Slay head into the bedroom where the second Iraqi man lies unconscious. They take his picture, and Ambush performs the process of facial-cloning analysis on Slay, who now looks exactly like the second official.

"Now you're going to see firsthand how our country ends up invading Iraq in the future."

Ambush and Ronnie exit the fourth-floor hotel suite.

"If anyone speaks to you, remain silent. I speak Arabic fluently, so let me handle any issues that should arise."

The elevator doors open, and they exit into a busy lobby full of international officials heading to the summit.

G-6's Agenda

No one at the conference seems to sense anything strange about Ambush or Slay masquerading as foreign officials. Ambush walks in first, because he knows exactly what he and Slay need to do to be seated. Two men approach them, identifying themselves as their aides and lead both imposters to their assigned seats. Ambush and Slay are given the itinerary for today's meeting.

"Uncle Bush, do you see what I see?"

"What is the problem, Ronnie?"

"The problem is on this itinerary."

"Are you referring to the Iraqi president being in attendance today?"

"That is exactly what I am referring to."

"What's your point?"

"The point is, we can kill this sleazebag today and change the future for the better."

Ambush quickly places his left hand on Slays' arm. "That's not going to happen, remember you didn't believe time travel real."

"Now you're gung ho?" Ambush whispers.

"You screw up here, you risk altering the present, and the future, we are here strictly to observe. Got it?"

Ambush squeezes Ronnie's arm and gives him an evil eye that would shame the devil.

An announcement comes across the intercom system in Arabic. All Iraqi officials in the conference room stand as their beloved leader enters and is seated.

The first thing discussed at the meeting is the matter of global oil prices. Chinese officials are very interested in the newly discovered oil supply that has graced the Nigerians, because China is in the process of building up their military infrastructure. A well-informed strategist knows, that to have a strong military, a huge supply of oil is a necessity. Since the Saudi Arabians are a close ally of the United States and supplies them 90 percent of their oil, the Iraqis plan to reduce the prices of their crude oil to destabilize the global market. This will cause economic hardship for the West, in the form of higher gas prices for the American people, leading to an enormous recession in America.

The plan is for the Nigerians to provide oil to the Chinese at a wholesale price, allowing the Chinese a window of opportunity to increase their military strength. This will send the message to the West that Iraq is considered a close ally of China and will not tolerate the Americans interfering in their affairs.

Another part of this global plot has the Chinese purchasing a huge sum of American savings bonds, giving them 15 percent ownership of the United States to speed up a recession in America the country won't soon recover from. A round of applause erupts; Ambush looks over at Slay as he lightly claps his hands and leans in close to him. "I suggest you clap your hands, Ronnie, or risk drawing unwanted attention to us."

Slay reluctantly lightly claps his hands. "This is some incredible shit, Uncle Bush."

Ambush scans the conference room to see if they are being watched. He feels it's time to return to the future before the delegates they're posing as wake up to sound the alarm.

"You've seen enough. The first chance we get, we're making our move to return to the future. Follow my cues."

Ambush begins coughing uncontrollably, interrupting the conference proceedings.

Slay assists Ambush to his feet and walks him out of the conference room. In Arabic, Ambush tells their aides he doesn't need their assistance; his partner is taking him out to get some fresh air. Summit security service officers follow them anyway. It's against protocol to let anyone unescorted move freely while the summit is in session. The security officers remain a small distance behind the two imposters.

Slay escorts Ambush into the men's room as he removes the T-3D. He programs the data for their return to Iraq, 1991.

A disturbance is unfolding at the elevators. The real dignitaries emerge into the hallway, still drowsy from the chemicals Ambush and Slay used on them. They tell security two foreigners entered their room, attacked them, and stole suits and their IDs; they believe the foreigners used their credentials to infiltrate the summit.

Security rushes toward the men's restroom. When they enter, they watch as Slay and Ambush enter a bright light in the shape of a door. They are frozen in place by the time vortex vacuum created when the door of light closes.

In the twinkling of an eye, the bright light vanishes.

In Iraq in 1991, a bright light in the shape of a door appears. Ambush and Ronnie emerge from the past, finding themselves back on the high-rise building, US marines frozen in place.

MY BEST FRENEMY

The rooftop doesn't look the same as it did before Slay embarked on his adventure and went back in time with Ambush. The giant air-conditioning unit position has been blown to bits; the rooftop door area is a pile of rubble. The frozen-in-place marines are soon moving on the rooftop once again, unaware they lost five minutes.

"What the hell happened here, Uncle Bush, while we were gone?"

"Whatever happened, be sure not to mention anything about traveling to the past to anyone you speak with, understood?"

"That's the last thing on my mind right now, Uncle Bush."

Slay walks over to a marine to find out what happened while he was in the past.

"Excuse me, Lieutenant."

The junior officer turns around, expecting to address a fellow marine, and instead finds himself face-to-face with a higher-ranking army officer.

"I would salute you, Captain, but I wouldn't want you to catch a hot one between the eyes."

The dark-green marine is tall and muscular, with gold paratrooper jump wings pinned on his battle dress top. He is unshaven, a half-smoked Cuban cigar in his mouth. He hasn't slept since arriving in Baghdad; his uniform has faded from being in the scorching sun for days.

"How did you get up here, sir? I don't recall seeing any army units accompanying us on our assault into the city."

"Ah, that's a story for another day, Lieutenant. You wouldn't believe me if I told you anyway."

The marine removes his cover[38] and uses it to wipe sweat from his face.

"Were you on the copter when my guys fast roped on the rooftop?

Slay shakes his head no to the marine's question. "Can you tell me what happened up here, Lieutenant?" Slay asks.

The marine begins to explain what unfolded on the rooftop. He tells Slay that a fierce firefight with the Iraqi Army erupted. His unit was moving through the streets at a steady pace before encountering strong resistance and enemy fire from light armored vehicle cannons, reinforced by RPGs,[39] trying to disable their tanks.

Suddenly, the rocket teams were being taken out by surgical sniper fire, he explains. He knew it wasn't one of his unit's snipers, because he is the officer in charge of the surveillance and target acquisition (STA) platoon. But he knew whoever it was, the godsent sniper was on their side.

Slay tunes out of the conversation momentarily and looks around, hoping to see Hunter emerge from among the

---

[38] Military term for headgear.
[39] Rocket-propelled grenades.

marines on the rooftop, displaying his trademark smile. He tunes back in to the explanation as the lieutenant tells Slay the sniper was the best he has ever seen. The sniper didn't miss; it was one and done.

The lieutenant explains that the Iraqis couldn't find the sniper's location until a Chinese attack copter showed up and blew the shit out of the rooftop. Slay's eyes widen after hearing that detail.

"Did you say Chinese copters?"

"Yeah, it was the craziest thing, a Hip and Hind Russian-style copter[40] swooped in, blowing the hell out of those huge air-conditioning units. And then the Hip copter hovered over the rooftop while Chinese troops fast roped onto the roof."

Slay removes his patrol cap and wipes his forehead with it. The marine credits the sniper for enabling him and his men to break the enemy's back. A squad of what he believes to be Iraqi troops rushed onto the rooftop through the roof door, followed by an explosion That explains the rubble where the rooftop door once stood. All this unfolded as the Chinese took the soldier who the marine believed was the unknown shooter into their custody.

Slay is sick to his stomach after hearing that Hunter was taken prisoner by the Chinese.

"What makes you think the shooter was taken by the Chinese, Marine?"

"Using my binos, I observed the letters *POC* inscribed on the copter's side. Do you know who that sniper was, Captain?"

---

[40] Attack and troop carrier helicopters made by Russia.

"I have my suspicions. Can you give me a description of the sniper?"

Slay hopes that the sniper wasn't Tony Hunter and that Tony was able to make an escape from the rooftop.

"Yeah, it was the strangest thing."

Slay hangs on every word coming from the marine's mouth, hoping for resolution.

"The guy had this crazy smile on his face. I mean, the guy was fearless. I thought, *Damn dude, semper fi*."[41]

The lieutenant's description of the sniper hits Slay like a nuclear bomb. It was Tony.

"Damn. Thanks for your help, Lieutenant. Best of luck to you and your men."

Since they're in a combat zone, instead of saluting Slay as the higher-ranking officer, the marine extends his hand toward Slay, and they shake hands. Slay, now in a depressive state of mind, walks slowly back to where Ambush is standing, finding the special agent on his sat phone.

"Yes, sir, I totally understand. This is a situation that has to be contained, yes, sir, at all costs. Out."

Ambush hangs up.

"Fuck me. How in the hell did the Chinese get their hands on one of our guys!"

Before he can finish his rant, Slay interrupts. "It's Tony, Uncle Bush."

"What about Tony? Where the hell is he? Did you catch up with him?"

"He's the POW."

---

[41] *Semper fidelis*, meaning "always faithful," is the motto of the US Marine Corps.

Slay fills Ambush in on what the marine told him. Ambush is at a loss for words; he tells Slay this is a result of the Chinese aligning with Iraq, as planned during the 1988 G-6 Summit. Never in a million years did Ambush think Hunter would become collateral damage as a POW.

Finally, the past has caught up with the present. China and Iraq are allies now. America invades Baghdad, and the Chinese respond by retaliating with military force, taking an American prisoner.

Captain Hunter, God be with you, Ambush thinks.

What makes things worse, nothing can be done about Hunter being taken prisoner, because the mission was a classified black operation. The United States will never acknowledge the existence of this mission or Captain Hunter.

AGENT SLAY

Ten years later, Ronnie Slay is thirty-two years old; he trades his military career in for a federal intelligence career and the title of special agent with the National Security Agency, known as No Such Agency.

The year is 2001. The Los Angeles Lakers win another NBA championship, defeating the Philadelphia 76ers in five games. America survives the hysteria of the new millennium's impending doom, when so-called experts prophesied that the technical world would collapse back into the dark ages because computer systems were incapable of reading numeral dates beyond 1999. This issue didn't occur.

Agent Slay is considered a seasoned veteran with the agency because he's gone on some of the most covert and dangerous classified missions in the world. His exemplary success rate as a clandestine operative is second to none.

Another impressive aspect about his career is that Agent Slay has been handpicked for the agency's relatively unknown Time-Travel Section Group Unit (TTSGU). There are only a handful of agents assigned to the group. Only the most trusted and outstanding agents can ever hope to be selected for this highly classified section of the NSA.

The history of the Time-Travel Section Group Unit dates to the Roswell incident, as explained in the rookie orientation documentary video. From the beginning, time-travel technology marked a major shift in global power for the agency and the United States. During this time, a law enforcement official reported seeing what is known today as a UFO (unidentified flying object) or UAP (unidentified aerial phenomenon).

Government authorities responded to the location and implemented a cover-up. All evidence was collected and taken to a secret military base in the middle of the desert run by the US Air Force.

Former president Harry Truman visited the classified base way out in the desert. Miles of early-warning devices surrounded the base as protection from curious sci-fi fanatics trying to access the military reservation. Several hangars concealed advanced aircraft from the public. These aircraft were only brought out in the middle of the night, because they were alien in origin.

Truman was shown the corpses of dead alien beings recovered at the Roswell site; the aliens appeared humanoid. The body and skull structures were like humans'; their skin tone was a light grayish color. The only major physical difference from humans was the lizard-like pupils, which could transform to humanlike pupils.

High-ranking military officials made a last-minute decision not to divulge evidence of having recovered living extraterrestrials, whom they referred to as "the Grays." They kept the fact they had living aliens in their custody a well-kept secret between themselves, not even informing the sitting president.

Stephen Michael

After observing the bodies of the dead extraterrestrials, the president came to the realization that we share the universe with other life-forms. He issued an executive order for the military officials to destroy everything having to do with the aliens. The president believed with every fiber of his being that if the American people got wind that their government had made contact with extraterrestrial life-forms, national and worldwide panic would erupt and be uncontainable. The floodgates to chaos and anarchy would open, never to be closed.

The president's executive order was ignored. Instead, military officials collaborated with the surviving extraterrestrials. They arranged to provide these aliens with whatever they desired in exchange for alien technology.

The extraterrestrials let it be known that people has a commodity they crave above anything in the universe: water. H_2O is to these aliens what oil is to humans; water is much needed to power their antimatter crafts. The aliens were in search of H_2O resources throughout the universe; after centuries of mismanagement, their H_2O resources had run dry. The aliens were an advance party from their mother ship, but their craft had run out of fuel. Now their craft was adrift in space, like a boat in the water without a paddle.

The aliens became disoriented when a severe meteorite storm thrust their spacecraft from the fourth dimension into the third dimension. They ended up in our solar system, and their spacecraft crashed on Earth.

This occurs when two planets in their solar system collide with one another.

It turned out to be a good stroke of luck for the extraterrestrials, because Earth offered a plentiful source of the water they needed badly. But not so good for humankind, because if the advance party of extraterrestrials was able to contact their mother ship, it would not have been in the best interests of Earth. An invasion would have taken place for the extraction of Earth's water resources.

Nothing on Earth would have prevented the extraterrestrials from taking over the planet, because the extraterrestrials have advanced weapon systems compared to humans' primitive ones. The extraterrestrials refer to humankind as a level 0^{42} civilization consciousness. They would have complete power to take over planet Earth, should they choose to do so, because humans harbor animosity, wage war, are extremely selfish, express hate, harbor contempt, and pursue worthlessness and nothingness. Humans are vain, covetous, and harbor distrust. They are swift to shed blood, harbor greed, love monetary gain, are fearful and evil by nature, and are easily divided against one another.

The opposite can be said about the aliens, from a level 4^{43} civilization consciousness, out of ten possible civilization levels that exist in the universe.

So, a decision was made by both species to work together for the best interests of both civilizations. The small group of military officials agreed to give these extraterrestrials unlimited access to Earth's H_2O resources in exchange for unlimited alien technology. Arrangements were made for a combined workforce between military service members and extraterrestrials who would function as technology

---

[42] A civilization consciousness just above Neanderthals.

[43] A civilization of advanced enlightenment consciousness.

consultants. They would conduct business on a highly classified installation known as Area 51

The US government still denies the existence of this base. During the Cold War, the American people were kept in a constant state of fear, by design. A fearful mindset kept the American public's attention on Cold War propaganda while the country accelerated in alien technology, with advancements in nuclear technology, computer science, advanced aircraft technology, satellites, cellular communications, spaceflight, planetary rovers, unmanned drones, stem cell research, DNA typing, GPS technology, stealth technology, laser systems technology, weather warfare (like the High-Frequency Active Auroral Research Program [HAARP]), mind control science, night vision and infrared technology, solar technology, robotics, wireless technology, and much more in the years to come.

The unsanctioned partnership with these aliens was solidified in upmost secrecy and brought about the creation of the Shadow Government Oversight Panel of Thirteen (SGOPT). The families that make up the SGOPT are some of the wealthiest and most powerful in America and throughout the world. This social elite class refers to the rest of humanity as sheeple, because they believe the masses are content with being told how to live their lives, happy to be herded through life without purpose, even willing to be led to the slaughterhouse via the wars the SGOPT creates to serve their needs and interests.

A treaty was drafted between the SGOPT and the extraterrestrials stating that government officials will give extraterrestrials access to Earth's H_2O resources. In return, the aliens pledge not to invade and take the planet over. The aliens also agree to provide their technology, on condition that it be shared with the rest of humanity and not be used for evil or hoarded for monetary gain.

To ensure proper use of the technology, the extraterrestrials give their human hosts the advanced technology in baby portions. They put a monitor-and-control system in place to control the technical growth of humanity, because of the biases and prejudices humans harbor toward one another. The extraterrestrials also consider humankind's history of atrocities perpetrated against one another. They are determined to make sure this agreement is honored. The aliens can read the minds of their human hosts. The extraterrestrials know that humankind is imperfect, evil by nature, and not to be trusted. This treaty stands to the present day.

Extraterrestrial representatives have been placed around the world in key leadership positions in every nation on Earth. They monitor human leaders in key positions of power with access to their technology. Should a violation occur that threatens the aliens' access to the planet's water resources, they will give the SGOPT a window of opportunity to solve the issue before they act, which won't end well for people.

An agreement was reached by both the SGOPT and the extraterrestrials to pursue time-travel technology first, because the technology can be useful in elevating the planet above level 0 civilization consciousness. It will enable humans to reverse horrific historical events inflicted against one another. It also gives humankind the ability to protect the past, secure the present, and preserve the future for the betterment of people, because their history is full of atrocities perpetrated against their own species.

These aliens are hopeful that humans will use the technology to reverse their tragic history, giving future generations an opportunity to elevate the planet above the current level 0 consciousness.

In actuality, the SGOPT really wants this technology to peer into time to learn how the future will look for the interests of their nation. If the future appears bleak for the United States and its allies, the SGOPT can use the new technology to alter the present and future in their favor. They really couldn't care less about the next generation's problems or about elevating the planet above a level 0 civilization consciousness.

The aliens are not surprised their human hosts are more interested in the technology for selfish purposes, but they cooperate with the humans to get the water they so badly need, like a drug addict needs dope to function.

The Time-Travel-Technology Development Group was created, located at an exclusive federal reservation at Seal Beach, Los Alamitos, California. The first T-3 agents were pioneers, known as time-travel-technology development pilots, or T-3DPs. Their mission was to test the alien technology for the agency, having no idea what to expect once they stepped into the unknown frontier of time travel.

Several T-3DPs went back into the past. Following protocol, they brought back physical artifacts from their assigned time period to confirm they were actually physically in that time period.

All the T-3DPs brought back artifacts, including a Revolutionary War rifle, a newspaper from the Great

Depression, a pilgrim traveler's hat, the Wright brothers' blueprints, Henry Ford's engine blueprints, an 1848-era gold nugget, Civil War garments, George Washington administration documents, Benjamin Franklin's key, and a copy of Lincoln's Gettysburg Address speech.

ENTER THE WHITE DRAGON

All the test pilot assignments to the past were a great success. The agency decided to donate all the trophies brought back by the T-3DPs to the Smithsonian Institute Museum, to avoid tempting agency staff to steal artifacts to make a profit.

Tragically, the agency lost a couple of T-3DPs who volunteered to travel into the future. In one situation, a T-3DP returned from the future with complete amnesia. He was never the same to his dying day.

Another test pilot mission to the future ended in a different way; a T-3DP never returned from the future. Agency suits figure the agent met with foul play or decided to remain in the future. He is classified as missing in action. The troubling aspect of his defection is he still has the T-3D in his possession.

Actually, the missing T-3DP was intrigued by how the future turned out; he decided to stay and use knowledge of past events to gain power and wealth.

Finally, the documentary ends. The flat-screen television fades to black. The lights come back on; every rookie assigned to the Time-Travel-Technology Unit (T-3D) appears sleepy. The total number of unit members is highly classified; not even the veterans, known as control agents (CAs), know this information. The agency implemented this security measure to prevent security breaches and espionage incidents in the unit.

All the rookies are about to meet their CAs. These veteran agents are the most experienced operatives in the unit and are responsible for training, grooming, and overseeing all progression of the rookies.

The chief of the unit enters the briefing room; all the rookies get to their feet. The chief was one of the original T-3PAs. It was his best friend who decided to go MIA and remain in the future. During that troubling period, the agency sent the chief on a classified search-and-recovery mission, to locate the UA (unauthorized absence) agent.

The chief successfully located his friend; unfortunately, he couldn't apprehend the rogue agent, because he would have had to risk his own safety in doing so. The rogues agent had obtained power and wealth that cushioned him from scrutiny.

"Gentlemen, take your seats. I want to welcome you all to the Time-Travel-Technology Unit. Our mission motto is to defend the past, protect the present, and preserve the future. You are now members of the most secretive and elite group, like no other in the world.

"All of you were handpicked for your outstanding records with the agency. Now you will be introduced to your CAs. Please address all questions to your CA. If your CA isn't able to find the answer to your issue, it will be brought to the director, and he will ensure that I apply my utmost diligence to find the answer to your questions."

Mild laughter fills the room.

"I wish you all much luck."

Moments later, several special agents enter the briefing room to introduce themselves to the rookies assigned to them. Slay hasn't been approached by any of the CAs yet. All of a sudden, he spots a familiar face in the crowd. The familiar face turns out to belong to none other than Talbert H. W. Ambush. He walks toward Slay; the senior agent hasn't seemed to age a bit since Slay last saw him. Besides the clean-shaven head, no one would know he was a decade older.

"How are you, Ronnie?"

They embrace.

"You sly fox—you're going to be my CA?"

"That I am. Sorry to disappoint you, buddy."

Slay grins widely. "Are you kidding? I'm not disappointed. As a matter of fact, I was concerned about who was going to be my CA. Some of these guys seem a little weird."

Both T-3 operatives laugh.

"I hate to break it to you—I'm as weird as you're going to find in this place."

Before Slay can ask Ambush the question that has been eating at him, his mind drifts off to days past.

It's 1989. After the last qualifying jump during airborne school, Hunter asks Slay what the next assignment in his military career will be.

"What's next for you in this big adventure, Ronnie?"

The two junior officers stand by to fall into formation

as Black Hat Army Ranger instructors account for all the airborne students. Ronnie removes his headgear before he responds to Hunter's question.

"I'm headed to Ranger School. What about you, brah?"

Hunter grins after hearing Ronnie's answer. "You're kidding me! No shit. Me too."

Slay's memories of the past fade away as the sounds of the other agent rookies and their handlers bring him back to the present. Ambush leads Slay to an unoccupied area in the briefing room. "You look like you have something heavy on your mind, Ronnie. Care to share?"

"Have you heard anything about Tony over the years?"

"Not a word. It's like he just fell off the face of the earth."

Slay lowers his head in disappointment. "I know if Tony had the smallest window of opportunity to escape from the Chinese, he wouldn't hesitate to bounce."

Ambush gently grabs his rookie by his left forearm. "You need to stop beating yourself up for what went down in Iraq years ago."

"I keep telling myself the same thing, but if I hadn't gone with you that day, Uncle Bush, things might be different today."

"Tony wanted to remain on that rooftop, remember?"

"Yeah, I remember, sir."

Ambush places his hands on Slay's shoulders. "My friends call me Uncle Bush; remember that too, right?"

"Yeah, I do, Uncle Bush."

"Focus. We have a lot of things to take care of today, so let's get started."

Later that day, Slay completes his processing into the unit and is given the group's mission statement. All necessary equipment, security clearances, and identification cards are secured by one of the newest members of the unit. Now he just wants to retire for the evening. Ambush suggests that Slay accompany him back to his residence so they can catch up on old times.

They arrive at Ambush's home. Both agents exchange war stories about their experiences in the field. Ambush tells Slay to follow him to the basement. Slay watches his CA pick up what he perceives to be a television remote. It turns out to be a remote to a quiet room, complete with soundproofing technology.

"I know us agency guys like secrecy, but don't you think this is a little overboard here, Uncle Bush?"

They laugh together. Ambush pushes a button on the remote, enclosing them in the quiet room.

"All jokes aside, Ronnie, I have some classified info. The agency has no idea I have this quiet technology, courtesy of the DIA.

"I can now answer the questions you asked me earlier. I was hesitant to answer them before because the agency walls have ears. If you ask the wrong questions, you could find yourself in violation of executive classified information protocol. Only the president of the United States and T-3U management are privy to such information."

Ambush explains the culture of the unit to Slay.

SHADOW WARRIORS

The Chinese intelligence agency takes its high-profile prisoners to the mountains of China. Many POWs from wars past, such as the Vietnam conflict, have ended up here. This explains why the US government could never locate missing service members from that decades-old conflict. When the United States launched recovery missions in an effort to find its service members in Southeast Asia and could not do so, it was because many of them had died from torture, neglect, and/or abuse by the Eastern Alliance offsite.

Today, in August 2001, the black site is updated with the latest in modern technology and is completely undetectable from America and its allies' satellite observation efforts. This is a strategic site where the Eastern Alliance operates its cyber-warfare attack campaigns against the United States and the West on a consistent basis, with complete impunity against discovery.

The Eastern Alliance has plans for Tony Hunter. After ten years of captivity, one would expect the American POW would be in bad shape, physically and mentally. But it's the opposite; he is in excellent health, body and mind, because the Eastern Alliance has treated him well to brainwash him for their purposes, when the time is right.

"Do you have a problem serving the interests of the people of China, comrade?"

"No, I have no problem serving the people of China, comrade."

"Very good. You have been of great use to the POC this past decade."

The foreign agent is referring to the sniper training Hunter has provided for their military. Because of his faithful service, the POC has decided to reward Hunter by assigning him to the ultra-secretive Time-Travel Reconnaissance Unit (TTRU). These intelligence agents are representatives from the relatively secret intelligence agency known as the Ministry of State Security (MSS). They obtained time-travel technology from an extraterrestrial species. Officials from the mainland came in contact with an alien life-form during the '70s on an oil-drilling platform off the cost of the East China Sea.

The aliens were described by officials as having scaly, reddish skin; glowing eyes; and two horse-like legs. These aliens possess high intelligence and are able to shape-shift into humanoid form. They took up residence on planet Earth, under the East China Sea, after a planetary disaster slingshot their spacecraft into Earth's solar system. They are known to the POC as the shape-shifting demons, highly advanced beings who communicate with their human hosts in mainland dialect.

The POC made a treaty agreement with these extraterrestrials; they agreed to provide the aliens whatever they desired in exchange for advanced technology.

The aliens have an insatiable lust for human plasma, so the POC agreed to provide human victims in exchange for their technology.

The POC handed over most of the remaining POWs to the aliens so that this shadow governmental arm of China would begin receiving the aliens' technology.

It has been ten years; Hunter has felt betrayed and abandoned by his country and, most surprisingly, by his dear friend Ronnie Slay. When Hunter reflects on more pleasant days with Slay, he recalls a funny moment years ago at Fort Benning, Georgia.

A colossal dark-green Ranger barks orders at the terrified airborne recruits. "If you took the time to read the footnotes on your new assignment orders, you would have read that you will be wearing your garrison caps while you attend Ranger School."

Slay looks over in Hunter's direction to discover that his friend is wearing the proper headgear; Slay is not. Hunter searches for Slay and finally spots him digging in his duffel bag, trying to locate his garrison cap.

"If you haven't already done so, you need to get your garrison caps on your domes ASAP! This will be the last time you will be told to get you heads out of your asses. As Rangers, you need to be leaders, and leaders don't need to be told what they should already know.

"Once you have removed those silly-looking raspberry berets from your domes, move your asses on the back of that deuce and a half and stand by to be transported to Camp

Darby to begin the journey others have failed to complete—trying to become Airborne Rangers!"

The MSS helps fan the flames of betrayal, despair, and abandonment Hunter now feels toward his country. This strategy is designed to win his unconditional loyalty to and cooperation with the POC. The MSS agents are aware that Hunter was on a covert mission years ago to assassinate Sheikh Khalid, a mission that, Hunter doesn't realize the United States denies even existed. This denial of the mission's existence is the main reason the US government never initiates a rescue attempt of Captain Hunter.

This situation plays into the hands of the MSS agents in their efforts to break Hunter, making sure that their prisoner loses all hope of ever being rescued by his country.

After concluding that he has been completely abandoned by his country, Hunter's mind becomes twisted with hatred for the United States and a special hatred for his colleague Ronnie Slay, who he believes threw their friendship away.

All that is in the past now. Hunter has new comrades and a new country. The people of China have treated him as a comrade, and he has embraced their humility.

"I swear my loyalty and allegiance to the service of the Eastern Alliance What would you have me do?"

The senior agent explains to Hunter he will be assigned to the TTRU; its mission is to manipulate the past, change the present, and control the future for global dominance for the East.

Hunter is given the task of reversing the assassination of Doctor Propaganda and reestablishing their plans to attack select major cities in the United States soon.

Back in America, in Ambush's quiet room, he and Slay continue their conversation about a possible future attack planned on US soil. The senior agent goes on to tell Slay he was assigned not long ago to verify a plot to attack the United States. It proved to be very frustrating for him because he kept coming up empty-handed, until an undercover mole informant from a hostile nation confirmed the source of the attack aimed at America.

According to intel, the attack, which is being planned by a time-travel operative from the East, will occur after another mission to reverse the assassination of Sheikh Khalid is launched.

"So, there are other nations with time-travel technology?"

Ambush crosses his arms in front of his chest. "Ronnie, this is a small world, but it's a huge universe. You can imagine other governments have contacted extraterrestrials like we did.

"My intel sources report that China is most likely the base of operations for the foreign agent who is tasked with reversing the assassination of Dr. Propaganda."

Slay asks Ambush if his contact had a picture or a name of this foreign agent. Ambush says there is no picture, but he did get the foreign agent's code name: the White Dragon.

Ambush explains the agency has assigned them to both go back in time to Iraq, 1991, to prevent the reversal of the assassination of Sheikh Khalid.

Early morning inside the agency's situation room, monitors on the wall show current affairs from around the world happening in real time. Ambush and Slay receive their mission operation orders. They gear up. Ambush is the lead agent, Slay the specialist. He is given the honor of activating the T-3D that will transport them both back to the year 1991.

A bright light in the shape of a door appears; both men step inside and vanish.

GHOSTS FROM THE FUTURE

On the rooftop of a high-rise building in Iraq, 1991, Ambush and Slay step out of a light from the future into the past. They scramble to the giant air-conditioning unit they occupied a decade before; the only thing missing is Tony Hunter.

The environment is eerie and quiet, just like it was on the original mission when Hunter made the shot that killed Dr. Propaganda. But now Hunter, the TTRU agent from the future known as the White Dragon, is on his way into the palace to warn Sheikh Khalid that his life is in danger. Hunter presents his MSS badge to the Iraqi Royal Guards and is given access to the building.

On the high-rise rooftop across the street, Ambush locates their target. This time Slay, instead of Tony Hunter, will take the shot that will kill Sheikh Khalid. There are some complications the two assassins didn't foresee. Ambush can't contact the F-117 stealth fighter pilots this time, because the authentication codes he used on the first mission don't exist anymore. If Slay fails to terminate the target, there won't be a secondary strike to ensure Sheikh Khalid is dead.

Ambush informs Slay to stand by; Slay confirms weapon

adjustment data and confirms he is ready to take the shot. Suddenly, Slay spots a second figure entering the kill zone. At first Slay thinks it's another Iraqi, but to his dismay, the second figure looks exactly like Tony Hunter. Slay doesn't say a word to Ambush, for fear the senior agent will think he has lost his mind.

Slay closes his eyes to gather his thoughts before pulling the trigger. He opens them to focus his crosshairs on the skull of his target. To his disbelief, the second figure appears to be his best friend, taken prisoner so many years ago. Hunter now turns and stares in his direction, displaying his trademark smile.

Slay's mind is consumed with the fog of confusion until he's interrupted by Ambush, who asks if he has confirmation on the target. Slay doesn't respond. He has been shaken to the core by seeing his best friend in the kill zone with his target.

Finally, he has proof that Tony is indeed alive, but instead of being on the rooftop with him and Ambush, Hunter is in the building with their target, trying to warn him that he is being targeted for an assassination. Everything seems a blur in Slay's mind.

Ambush suspects that something is troubling his rookie. Immediately he raises his binoculars to observe the kill zone, and he spots an individual resembling Tony Hunter in the same room with their target. Ambush stays focused and gives Slay the command.

"Take the shot—take it now!"

Slay concentrates on the crosshairs of his scope, steadying the sight on Sheikh Khalid's temple as he exhales and squeezes the trigger. The weapon fires a live round downrange.

The assassination is spoiled by Hunter. He pulls Sheikh Khalid to the floor before Slay's full-metal-jacket round can reach its target. On the street, palace guards immediately radio the quick-reaction team. The team scrambles across the street and enters the high-rise building, en route to the rooftop.

The team reaches the rooftop entrance and breaches the locked door with a shotgun slug, unaware the door is rigged with plastic explosives. The C-4 ignites, causing a huge explosion and killing most of the team members in place.

On the opposite side of the door, Agents Ambush and Slay are taken by surprise by the explosion. The concussion tosses both to the ground. Ambush manages to activate the T-3D, returning him and Slay to the year 2001. The surviving Iraqi team members are frozen in place by the time vortex that the portal causes. Slay and Ambush step out of the bright light into present-day America.

The White Dragon, a.k.a. Tony Hunter, takes control of the chaotic scene after the attempted assassination on Sheikh Khalid. The Eastern Alliance operative informs the grateful Doctor Propaganda that the MSS has a message for Iraqi to relay to his leader.

Sheikh Khalid's body language betrays his calm demeanor. Hunter hands him a US twenty-dollar bill that carries a hidden code only the conspirators are aware of. The twenty has been folded in such a way that it displays an image of two very tall buildings on fire, with smoke emitting from them. This is the secret code Sheikh Khalid and the POC created some time ago, the signal for sleeper cells to initiate their plans of attack against America on US soil.

Intel reports are coming in that American forces are on the outskirts of Baghdad, destroying everything in their way and eliminating top Iraqi officials. Hunter advises Sheikh Khalid to flee Baghdad so that he'll be able to deliver the occult message to the Iraqi leadership immediately. Before letting him go, as directed by the MSS, Hunter takes a photo of Sheikh Khalid with the time stamp 1991 on it, to verify he was successful in preventing the assassination of the Iraqi official.

After ensuring the escape of Sheikh Khalid, Hunter returns from the past to the future in the blink of an eye, to the POC intelligence black site. His Chinese handlers debrief him as a Russian SVR[44] agent looks on.

"I take it that your mission was a complete success, comrade?"

Hunter renders a bow of respect to the Russian agent as is customary in his new culture.

"Yes, comrade, the mission was a great success. Sheikh Khalid is alive and well." Hunter removes his time-travel device and hands it to the Russian intelligence agent. They all observe the picture of Sheikh Khalid holding the folded twenty-dollar bill, along with a manila envelope, time-stamped 1991.

"Yes, Dr. Propaganda is very much alive. You have done yourself, China, and our allies a great service, my Yankee comrade. It won't be long before the Americans and their way of life are crippled. We will attack their homeland, which of course is just a diversion to keep American resources busy for some time. Then we will execute the real plan—seizing global power and complete rule of the planet."

All agents, including Hunter, laugh out loud.

---

[44] Russia's version of America's NSA.

BURNING TOWERS OF BABEL

I n 2001, Ambush and Slay are debriefed by T-3U Senior
Agent Hutton.

"So, you had Sheikh Khalid in your sights, but he
escaped because your best friend, whom you served with
in the Ranger regiment, showed up to save that sorry sack
of shit at the last minute? Is that what you would have me
believe, rookie?"

Slay smirks slightly after receiving the verbal assault
from the irate agency suit. "Not in those words, but yes.
Tony Hunter showed up and compromised the mission."

Slay takes a moment to wipe sweat away from his face;
the expression on Agent Hutton's face is worth a million
words.

"A fucking ghost from your past pops up on a covert
operation—not to mention the mission is unfolding in
the fucking past, which means this asshole has time-travel
capabilities. He prevents the assassination of one of the worst
genocidal maniacs to have ever walked the planet. This is
what I have to report to the fucking director?"

Slay is at a loss for words, so he only nods slowly in
response to Agent Hutton's comment. Hutton has everyone

turn their attention to the giant supercomputer monitor. He then feeds information about the compromised mission into it to find out how the future was altered due to the failed mission. The situation computer processes the information. The conclusions are chilling.

Splashed across the flat-screen monitor is a scene of major American cities under attack, buildings burning, people running in mass chaos and panic. The screens fades to black as the lights come back on.

"Because you couldn't do your fucking job, you placed American citizens in jeopardy. Are you good with that, Agent Slay?"

Slay is annoyed by Agent Hutton's verbal assault and is ready to give the same back. "You have one more time to yell at me like I am a fucking child before you see a side of me you won't like … sir."

"What did you fucking say to me, rookie?"

Without delay, Ambush weighs in on the heated conversation. "Wait a minute, sir. I believe what Agent Slay is trying to say is that fatigue and back-to-back deployments have affected his judgment. Isn't that right, Agent Slay?"

Ronnie Slay gazes at Ambush in confusion but goes along with the bullshit story spewing out of his CA's mouth. Ambush raises his eyebrows to suggest that Slay go along with his story, if he knows what's good for him.

"Ah—right. It's been really hard on me, a decade of not knowing what happened to Captain Hunter, what happened to my best friend. So, like Agent Ambush said, my mind played tricks on me."

Agent Hutton folds his arms across his chest in disgust and cuts a look of frustration in the direction of Ambush, who just shrugs his shoulders at the agency suit as Slay continues his explanation during the debrief.

"My judgment was affected, and I missed my target, sir."

Realizing that his senior CA just bought his rookie a loophole excuse, Hutton uncrosses his arms, a stern smirk on his face. "Now that explanation I can swallow. I'll tell you this one time and one time only, rookie. If you want to remain a member of the T -3U, I suggest you get your head out of your ass."

Then he slams his fist on the table in front of Ambush. "I'm recommending that you have your rookie visit our shrink before he goes on any more missions. Is that understood?"

Ambush chuckles at Agent Hutton's weak attempt at intimidating him. "You got it, Hutton—right away, sir."

"Make it happens yesterday," Hutton says as he exits the briefing room.

Ambush signals for Slay to remain silent by placing his right index finger to his lips; the agency has hidden microphones everywhere.

Later that day, downtown in the city, young urban professionals casually cruise the streets in an effort to score some coke and weed to party with later, when they retire from their corporate nine-to-fives. Young hustlers provide their yuppie customers with their fixes and count their money. Other street events unfold like a well-oiled machine running on all cylinders without losing a beat. Young girls, turned out sexually by their pimps, get into strangers' cars to engage in perverted sexual intercourse for pay. Corrupt cops, paid well by the pimps, look on and do nothing.

Stephen Michael

Ambush and Ronnie sit in the back of a sleazy bar discussing what went wrong during their mission.

"I bet Hutton is good at swallowing a lot of stuff," Slay says.

Ambush chugs beer straight out a pitcher instead of from his mug. "Don't take his ass chewing personally. That's what suits do, Ronnie my boy."

Despite harboring disappointment toward his rookie, Ambush understands that he must be patient as Slay adjusts to the unit.

"Hey, Ronnie, what really happened to you on the roof?"

Slay slowly sips his mug of beer.

"Tell me why you really fucked up on the mission."

"Uncle Bush, do you trust me with your life?"

Ambush leans forward.

"I trust you with my life, Ronnie. You know that."

Slay finishes the rest of the dark beer in his mug before responding. "Then trust my judgment too."

Ambush takes a long gulp from his pitcher, finishing what was left of the beer, and slams a now-empty pitcher on the table.

"All I know is that you had Sheikh Khalid in your sights, and you failed to assassinate that scumbag."

Slay lowers his head in shame as he reflects on the fact he did the right thing by not firing on the person he believed to be Tony Hunter.

"All we can do now is sit and wait for the fallout and see how our failure will alter the future."

Both men finish their meals and head to their homes for a long, sleepless night, not knowing what the future may hold for them and the entire world.

The year 2001 is filled with many memorable events. An American is executed for carrying out one of the worst domestic terrorist acts in US history in the state of Oklahoma. That summer becomes known as "the summer of the shark" after numerous shark-attack fatalities occur in America. The mayor of Cincinnati declares a state of emergency after several riots break out in his city as protests the acquittal of a white cop who killed an unarmed black youth erupt. All those events will pale in comparison to what is about to unfold later in 2001 in America.

Early in the morning on September 11, 2001, people go about their business as usual until a passenger plane slams into one of New York City's Twin Towers, the symbol of America's financial strength. Most of the people on the ground think it's a freak accident of some kind, until a second plane slams into the other tower, and then panic ensues as chaos erupts on the ground below.

After being exposed to intense fire, one of the towers begins to collapse, sending an enormous cloud of debris rushing through the streets of New York City.

Elsewhere in the skies above, somewhere in America, terrorists have hijacked a second plane, destination unknown. Military command scrambles fighters after a third hijacked plane fails to respond to air traffic controllers' radio transmissions. An executive order is given to bring the third plane down, reported to be headed to DC with the goal of slamming into the White House.

Fighter jets shoot the second hijacked plane down over an open area in Pennsylvania; the aircraft and everyone on board are vaporized by untraceable silicone missiles. The media reports that passengers on board overtook the terrorist, causing the hijackers to lose control of the plane and crash. That would answer the questions that arose about why there weren't any visible signs of plane wreckage debris or bodies in and around the crash site.

Streaking through the sky, the third hijacked plane speeds toward the Pentagon and slams into the military complex. This crash site is also questionable, with no visible proof of plane wreckage or corpses strewn around the Pentagon. Rumors rise that the incident was a false-flag operation the SGOPT put in motion to shock the American people into agreeing to invade Iraq.

In his residence in Manhattan Beach, California, Ronnie Slay watches the special news report in horror as the first tower collapses violently to the streets below in New York City. Talbert H. W. Ambush also watches the horrific scene on his television. Suddenly he receives a call on his secured cellular phone, dedicated to foreign intelligence resources.

"Listen, and don't say a word. I have only a moment. Today's attack is just a diversion. Hostile nations and their allies plan to travel back in time to reverse the assassination of JFK; their agenda is to seize global power.

"This will usher in a new order of oppression never known by humanity. They must be stopped at all costs. If they are successful in reversing this historical event, the free world will be a thing of the past."

Ambush tries to press the double agent for more details, but the line goes dead. Ambush speed-dials Slay.

"Now we know how our failure has affected the future."

"My God, Uncle Bush, what have I done?"

"Don't beat yourself up, kid; we have more-urgent

matters to deal with. I just received an anonymous call on my secured cell. This attack is just the tip of the iceberg of a more sinister plot that will destabilize the entire world. Gear up and meet me at the agency. I will catch you up on what lies ahead of us."

At the secret satellite agency compound in Seal Beach, Los Alamitos, California, Agents Ambush and Slay sit in an agency's situation room; Ambush fills his rookie in on the complete situation behind the attacks that happened earlier. He tells Slay this has all been verified by a reliable source working from the inside of enemy intelligence agencies throughout the world.

NEW WORLD DISORDER

Ambush tells Slay the attack on the country is a diversion to tie up American resources for as long as possible so the perpetrating nations can execute their real plan, which is to launch a worldwide coup, resulting in global domination. Ambush informs Slay that foreign agents are being sent on a mission to travel back in time to 1963, to Dallas, Texas. Their mission is to reverse a major historical event—the assassination of one of this country's revered leaders, JFK. Slay asks how preventing the assassination of JFK can pose a threat to the United States.

"I don't know, but we're going to find out."

Ambush feeds data into the situation computer, which processes the information and uploads the results on the giant flat-screen monitor. According to the supercomputer, should the Eastern Alliance[45] succeed in reversing the assassination of JFK, they will alter the future of America and the entire world in this way: America's global power is no more; Russia aids China in taking over all of Asia,

---

[45] The coalition of Eastern sovereignties working together to take over the world.

except North Korea; North Korea, with China's aid, overthrows South Korea; Africa is taken over and renamed New Nigeria; Iraq overthrows and rules the Middle East; Nicaragua overthrows all of Latin America except for Mexico; a huge number of American combat forces are wiped out; reinforcements arrive from China's First Naval Battle Group, which defeats American and Mexican forces on the border of California; Russia overthrows all of Europe, Canada, and Alaska; Russian and Chinese special forces overthrow all states bordering Canada, wiping out a huge chunk of American ground forces. All these events come to pass after the reversal of the assassination of JFK.

The screen fades to black, and the lights turn back on automatically. Ambush and Slay sit in momentary silence. Ambush displays a grim look on his face before speaking.

"The situation computer just showed us that the world as we know it will come to an end if this foreign agent succeeds in reversing the assassination of JFK."

Slay looks bewildered, not just because of the shock of America being stripped of global influence but also because of the fact that his parents and loved ones will meet horrific deaths when hostile nations attack Montana, his home state, which abuts the Canadian border. Slay closes his eyes briefly, then speaks.

"We can't allow this catastrophe to occur."

Ambush slowly gets out of his chair and walks around the table, stopping in front of Slay before weighting in.

"The irony of the whole situation is that we're talking about going back in time to ensure that JFK is assassinated. That's the saddest thing about the whole situation. But if we do nothing, the country JFK helped shape will be destroyed and replaced with hostile nations that will turn our country into a nation of oppressed people."

The whole situation is tragic to Slay, especially the part about Russia taking over the states bordering Canada. He reflects to a moment he spent with his parents during better times.

Ronnie Slay Sr. let's go of his son and looks at his wife before giving her a kiss on the cheek and letting her have a moment with their son.

"Ronnie, I'm so proud of you, and I've had such a great time spending the day with you today at Fort Benning," she says.

Ronnie holds both of his mother's hands. "Me too, Mom. I'm glad you and Dad could make it here today."

Mrs. Slay gently touches her son's cheeks. "Are you kidding? We wouldn't have missed it for the world. You look so handsome in your red hat."

Ronnie laughs out loud at his mother's comment. "Mom, it's not a hat! It's called a beret."

Mrs. Slay grins at her son. "Beret, hat—it doesn't matter. What matters to me and your father is that our son has become a man, no matter what you may have on your head.

"Remember: from sunrise to sunset, you are Ronnie Slay. Don't get caught up in an attachment to symbols and badges. They don't validate who you are. You validate who you are by your actions and by keeping your word as a man to others. Remember this, Ronnie, and you will never have to prove yourself to anyone."

Ronnie looks in his mother's olive-green eyes and replies, "Okay, Mom, I'll remember that. I promise."

Reality interrupts Slays' memory of his parents that seems like a lifetime ago. He knows there won't be other memories of his folks to look forward to if the T-3U fails to ensure the hostile T-3D operative doesn't reverse the history of JFK's assassination—nothing except living in bondage under the oppressive rule of the Eastern Alliance, which will usher in a godless, antagonist new world order.

Ambush puts together a rapid-deployment team to try to locate the foreign agent's base of operations. Slay is tasked with traveling to future America to conduct a time-travel reconnaissance (TTR) mission to verify whether the United States will be engulfed in a war with Eastern Alliance forces. Should Slay find these facts to be true, his mission will confirm that the foreign agent has already traveled back in time to 1963 to begin to sabotage the past. Then it will be up to Ambush and Slay to ensure JFK's assassination isn't manipulated to prevent a future attack on the United States and its allies.

Agent Slay is provided with credentials that will assist with providing him cover once he arrives in America's future. Should he find himself surrounded by enemy forces, Slay will have credentials identifying him as a member of the international press corps. If he finds himself among friendly forces and allies, he will have credentials as a secret service agent.

Back in the mountainous region of China, mission discussions are being held with Russian SVR agents who have in their possession a top secret, highly classified file on JFK. This file contains facts about him that the KGB accumulated during his administration. This secret documentation exposes certain activities JFK orchestrated or would have orchestrated had he not been assassinated. These plans can be neither confirmed nor denied. JFK intended to withdrawn US forces from Vietnam and scrapped the nuclear arms race with Russia. JFK wanted to break up the CIA (because of his great contempt for Richard Heelms). He abandoned CIA operatives in Cuba (in relation to the Bay of Pigs operation) and would have exposed the illegal activities of the FBI's Counter Intelligence Program (COINTELPRO), including the targeting of Martin Luther King Jr., the Honorable Minister Malcolm X, the Black Panther Party, and other US citizens. JFK also would have provided aid to Arab countries, helping them to build up their military infrastructure, which would threaten Israel's national security. Due to his discovery that the Federal Reserve prints worthless currency and charges interest out of thin air, making the US a debtor nation to a group of corrupt international bankers, he would have abolished the Federal Reserve System. As per his Executive Order 11110, he would have created debt-free currency to take the place of the Federal Reserve note. He double-crossed the American mafia. After the Chicago mob helped JFK win the White House, RFK went after the mob as the attorney general. Finally, JFK would have signed the civil rights bill and exposed the existence of the SGOPT.

All these executive plans threatened the national security of the United States. JFK knew this and didn't care, because he was determined to win the White House for a second term by any means necessary; he answered to no one and to no group. He was determined to fulfill his agendas and set himself up as the first American king.

If he hadn't been assassinated, all these policies would

have given the United States' enemies the edge for global power. With the ability to time travel, the playing field can now be leveled in favor of nations that hate America.

Currently at Seal Beach, Los Alamitos, California, unit suits go over last-minute details with Agent Slay before the rookie conducts a time reconnaissance of future America.

"Remember, Agent Slay: when you arrive in future America, you are there strictly to observe and report. Do not interfere in any way with events, or you will alter time. Any questions?"

A certain classified document in the agency's eyes' only files explains the early days in the human and extraterrestrial working relationship.

The SGOPT uses T-3D capabilities to learn the identities of future US presidents. These T-3D reconnaissance programs begin after the Truman administration.

Future America will sit its first African American President in US history; in the not-too-distant future, a woman and a Reality icon businessman will run for the highest office in the land, with a real estate mogul becoming the first sworn-in Commander in Chief, whose motto is: 'Make America Great Again.'

During the mission brief, Slay is told that should he find America under siege by foreign military forces, most likely martial law will be in effect, so having Secret Service credentials will help keep Ronnie Slay from possibly being shot on sight for violating martial law.

Being a T-3D rookie means Slay feels a little nervous. But still, Ronnie Slay is true to form as he prepares himself to witness a future America that sounds dangerous and intriguing.

THE GREAT DRAGON

W hen Ronnie Slay activates his T-3D, a bright, door-shaped light appears; he is transported to future America in the twinkle of an eye.

Somewhere in time, Slay steps out into America's future shock. The T-3D rookie feels like he's on the streets in an Iraqi war zone. Buildings are on fire, and there is little to no civilian activity on the streets. There are military checkpoints on most street corners. He can hear artillery shells exploding in the distance, followed by pockets of small arms fire. He thinks, *Holy shit, is this America?*

Slay begins recording the activities on his T-3D, gathering intel for the suits for when he returns from America's embattled future.

Before Slay can react, a couple of US marines aggressively advance upon him, their weapons pointed in his direction.

"Hey, asshole, why are you on the fucking streets? Get your fucking hands up now!"

The higher-ranking Marine points the muzzle of his weapon at Slay; the T-3D operative is careful to follow all instructions given.

Both marines physically slam him to the ground. One of

the marines starts to search him. The other keeps the muzzle of his weapon pointed at Slay's head.

"Don't you fucking move! I will blow your fucking brains out all over the streets!"

The marine searching Slay slams his knee in the middle of Slay's back.

"Take it easy. I'm with the Secret Service."

The marine conducting the search finds Slay's credentials. The marines both lower their weapons immediately, allowing Slay to get his feet.

"No hard feelings, sir—just following orders. You do know martial law is in effect, right?"

An artillery round strikes a commercial building in the distance and explodes. Slay notices that the marines barely react to the impact of the shell; they are battle-tested, just like him.

"Foreign forces are shelling the outskirts of Bethesda," one of the marines says.

Finally, Slay has received confirmation of his location in future America.

"So, this is Maryland?"

The marines give each other quick glances. Both marines chuckle under their breath at the strange behavior of the Secret Service agent.

"Yes, sir. This is Maryland."

Slay realizes he sounds like a fruit loop, something he should avoid.

"Chinese marines have taken over the Eastern Shore and are advancing toward Washington, sir."

Slay borrows a radio from one of the marines so he can request a copter to fly him to Washington, DC. A

Blackhawk helicopter arrives to pick him up. Because a no-fly zone has expanded around the White House, the closest the copter crew can take him is the outskirts of Washington.

After Slay makes contact with the Secret Service command, an escort detail picks him up and takes him to the White House, where Slay is verified and confirmed as the commander of the Secret Service's northern counterassault team (CAT), special weapons and tactics (SWAT) unit. There is no way to dispute who Ronnie Slay really is, because all Secret Service agents in the northern region command have been wiped out by enemy forces.

Slay is asked to tell them anything he can about the situation unfolding up north. Using the intel provided to him before he was transported to future America, Slay informs the White House staff that foreign antagonist forces have successfully taken over all states bordering Canada. They occupy and control the Canadian border. The White House staff had no way of discovering this information on their own because enemy forces have managed to knock out all observational satellites, blinding the US military. With a heavy heart, Slay tells the staff that 99 percent of American forces along the Canadian border have been wiped out.

The foreign invaders plan to continue the assault down from the north and link up with enemy naval forces from Maryland's Eastern Shore for an assault on the White House. The entire staff erupts in loud discussions.

A National Security Council official approaches Slay to ask him if he would be willing to go north to conduct a recon. The official says they could use some real-time intelligence to learn the enemy's movements, what military weaponry they have at their disposal, and so on. Slay agrees to go on the strategic reconnaissance mission, not just to gather intelligence but also to try to contact his parents. Just the thought of his parents possibly being in enemy-held territory causes his heart to pound in his chest.

An aircraft transports T-3U operative Slay to the drop zone for his strategic reconnaissance mission. High above the state of Montana, Slay reflects on the time he first met his best friend, Tony Hunter.

"Hey, asshole, get the fuck off my chute before you kill us both!"

Suddenly Slay feels something odd on the bottom of his boots. He looks down and realizes he is on the canopy of a fellow Airborne student's chute. Slays' rate of descent increases, and he looks up to observe that his chute is fast collapsing on top of him. Without hesitation, Slay moves as fast as his legs will allow him to scramble off of the canopy below him.

Slay free-falls twenty-five feet before his chute redeploys, decreasing his rate of descent. Second Lieutenant Slay is relieved when his chute redeploys, and he yells out loud, "Damn, that was fucking crazy!"

Tony Hunter, the student jumper whose chute Slay was on, is now to his left, about fifty meters away.

"Are you fucking stupid or something? You trying to get us both killed before we get our jump wings, asshole?"

Slay looks in the direction of the yelling to observe Second Lieutenant Hunter's silhouette.

"Hey, sorry about that, dude. I had no idea I was on your chute."

Slay's memory of that comical encounter with Hunter comes to an end when the command to stand by to exit the aircraft is announced.

Agent Slay executes a HALO jump; he free-falls for a period, and then his chute deploys. After he safely lands on the ground, he finds himself in a state of shock at the condition of his hometown. Buildings are engulfed in flames, houses are leveled, and hundreds of corpses are sprawled all over for as far as Slay can see.

He slowly uses the communication satellite device to contact American forces for a rendezvous pickup. After shaking off the fog of shock brought on by the condition of his beloved hometown, he realizes that he is a sitting duck for possible enemy detection. He quickly moves into the woods for cover until he can be picked up.

In the distance, the T-3U rookie operative hears the sound of mechanized vehicles, which he assumes is his ride from American forces. He decides to error on the side of caution and stays in his concealed position. This proves to be the right decision; soon he observes enemy forces approaching. A couple of light armored vehicles move past, followed by dismounted enemy troops.

They stop near his concealed position to set up a temporary base camp, which complicates things for the T-3 rookie. If he decides to flee, he could be captured or, worse, killed. The T-3 rookie thinks of activating his T-3D and trying to make his escape. But he knows he has a mission to accomplish that is vital for the protection of the past, security of the present, and preservation of America's future. So, he stands down on the thought of retreat.

OPERATION ARMAGEDDON

In the distance, Slay hears what he believes to be copters approaching his position. Before the enemy can react, explosions erupt all around their location, blowing up the light armored vehicles. Machine-gun fire cuts the enemy troops to shreds. They didn't stand a chance against two Apache attack helicopters.

Slay tosses a green-smoke grenade out in the open to identify himself as an ally and avoid being fired upon. He uses the call sign that identifies him to the copter pilots as the package to be extracted. He is told to move to the unimproved road west of his position, to be picked up by a S tryker[46] unit.

After he is picked up, Slay learns that enemy forces have destroyed most of the state of Montana. He arrives at a missile silo base that has been converted into a temporary command post for what is left of American forces operating in the northern region.

American citizens who haven't been killed have been taken captive. The condition of Helena, the capital of

---

[46] Elite US Army mechanized unit.

Montana, is undetermined; resisting private citizens and police officers there inflicted a lot of damage on the enemy.

Slay requests that he be taken as close to Helena as possible to complete his strategic reconnaissance mission for Washington. His deepest hope is really to confirm that his parents haven't been captured or, worse, killed.

Near the end of the day, Slay finds himself outside the acreage of his family's farm estate. Considering the circumstances, you wouldn't know his hometown was under siege; the family home and property are undisturbed and unoccupied by enemy forces. Slay desperately wants to approach his parents' residence, but he doesn't. He dreads the thought of possibly discovering that his parents are dead.

Ronnie reflects to the conversation he had with his parents after he decided to join the military. A smile appears on his face as he recalls his mother telling him to write on a regular basis from OCS and how his dad was clowning around, telling him to have smart eyes and to kill the enemy before they could kill him.

Never in a million years did he think his parents would be in danger from enemy forces in his hometown, of all places. The T-3U rookie must remind himself, *This is future America*. He finds comfort in knowing that in present-day America his parents are safe and sound.

Slay remembers the day he walked away from the love of his life to join the military.

Tammy gives Slay a disappointed expression. "When were you going to tell me that you planned on joining the US Army? Didn't you think I deserved to be told what your plans were?"

Ronnie shrugs his shoulders at Tammy's question. "Not really. I'm going into the army, and you can't go with me. It's just that simple. We've had an on-and-off relationship since we were nine years old, Tammy. Did you really think we would walk down the aisle or something?"

It's apparent that Ronnie's words hurt Tammy's feelings deeply.

"I thought maybe we would grow closer over the summer and then get an apartment together."

Ronnie walks to where Tammy is standing and takes her hands in his. "In a perfect world that sounds great, but you and I both know in a matter of months we would be at each other's throats, and the battle of the sexes would be on and popping."

They both laugh out loud together as tears run down Tammy's cheeks.

It's dusk when it dawns on Slay that he can call Tammy, as she told him she would never change her cell number so that he could always get in touch with her. Tammy is shocked to the core when she receives a call from Ronnie Slay. She tells him enemy troops have killed numerous people; a lot of them are people she and he grew up with. She also tells him she wishes he were there to protect her. Slay tells her he is just outside his family's estate, and she gets excited. Her high school sweetheart is not only alive and well, but he's back in their hometown. Tammy gives Slay a bit of good news: his parents are at her place, safe and sound.

Later, Slay is approximately a hundred meters away from Tammy's house, concealed in the woods, when he calls Tammy a second time to avoid being mistaken for the enemy and shot. Tammy leans out of the second-story window of her home to let Slay know it's safe for him to come in.

As soon as Slay enters Tammy's house, his parents embrace him, kissing him on his cheeks and forehead.

"Oh, my God. Mom, Dad, I'm glad to see you."

Slay hasn't seen his parents since joining the military. Now add twelve more years on top of that. He must remind himself that he is in the future. Both his parents have gray hair now. They continue to embrace their only child as if it is their last day on earth.

Finally Slay comes face-to-face with Tammy and is smitten by how beautiful she has become. He can't help but admire the curvy, sexy figure she has grown into. They embrace. Slays' thoughts are along the lines that he may have made a mistake by joining the service instead of settling down to marry his high school sweetheart.

Tammy's house is occupied by several other people from around the area who lost their homes to the destruction enemy forces inflicted during the initial invasion of Helena. Nearly all the men are armed with pistols or semiautomatic weapon they managed to salvage from their homes. The T-3D rookie is told the enemy forces haven't overthrown the surrounding areas yet, because they're busy trying to secure the capital.

Later, Slay finds himself alone with his father, discussing the good old days.

"Ronnie, I can't tell you how good it is to see you alive and well. Your mother and I have been worried sick about you, we has not heard from you in twelve years."

Slay cracks a slight grin. "I apologize, Dad. A lot of things have happened to me since I last saw you and Mom.

I work for the federal government now, and they have me crazy busy much of the time."

Tammy enters the room accompanied by a man who turns out to be her fiancé. She introduces him to Slay. After her fiancé leaves the room to help fortify the backyard with a couple of other men, Slay tells Tammy that she has done well for herself. He says he could kick himself in the ass for letting her get away. She tells Slay all is not lost. If he decides to stay in Montana, there's a good chance he could win her heart back, because she has never stopped loving him. He is flattered, but he tells her he works for the government now and would never be home, which wouldn't be fair to her.

Outside, far in the distance, artillery explosions can be heard, a sinister reality enemy forces are getting closer to the outskirts of Helena. The T-3U rookie finds himself at a crossroads. In the back of his mind, part of him wants to stay. He has a ready-made family with Tammy, and his parents have aged gracefully and are healthy.

Slay is torn between the dilemma of whether to stay or return to present-day America. If he stays, the agency will figure he was killed or captured or, worse, has become a traitor who decided to stay in the future for selfish reasons.

Slay thinks, *Can I live with myself, knowing that my decision will cause the deaths of hundreds of millions of people in future America? Not to mention the destruction of the greatest nation to have ever graced the face of the earth?*

Betrayal is not an option for Ronnie Slay; it is clear to him what he most does.

It isn't long before Slay returns to Seal Beach, Los Alamitos, California, in present-day America, in the twinkle of an eye.

America under Siege

Agent Slay is debriefed by agency suits; he confirms their worst fears, verifying that the future holds a dreadful reality for the United States and its allies. The Eastern Alliance is in the process of taking over the planet by reversing a historical event.

The brass informs Slay that his next mission operations order brief will not happen until Agent Ambush returns from his own TTR assignment.

Somewhere in Hong Kong, Talbert H. W. Ambush makes his way on board a fishing boat to hold a secret conference with a foreign asset who is in reality an extraterrestrial watcher, an extraterrestrial monitor who keeps an eye on nations with alien technology to deter them from abusing the technology.

"Welcome to my humble fishing vessel, Uncle Bush."

After welcoming the T-3U operative carrying a briefcase aboard the decoy boat, the extraterrestrial renders a bow of respect to Ambush, who returns the same. The fishing vessel heads out to sea. Both of them sit quietly, enjoying the calm of the sea; they have a beautiful view of the Hong Kong shore from their position on the water.

After traveling far enough out to sea, the alien says, "It's been a long time, Uncle. I trust you have something for me?"

Without delay, Ambush presents the briefcase and opens it, exposing several bags of blood plasma. The extraterrestrial picks up one of the bags of plasma.

"I take it these are AB negative, my friend?"

"Aren't they always?"

The extraterrestrial returns the bag of plasma to the briefcase and closes it.

"This new supply of plasma will be used to continue our hybrid-human cloning project, which has been very successful since the '50s. Looking at you reinforces how successful the project has become."

Ambush smirks slightly at the alien's comment.

"I trust that no one at the agency has any idea you are a hybrid human, do they, Uncle?"

"Our secret remains just that, our little secret, Zendora."

"That's good to know, because the watchers don't want a repeat of what occurred in Berlin in the 1930s, when the Germans betrayed our trust and tried to create a master race using our hybrid cloning technology.

"They lost track of the fact our civilization is here to elevate this planet from its current level 0 existence to a level 1 or higher existence."

Ambush lets out a slight yawn; he has heard this same story from the alien monitor every time they meet.

"I need some intel on a possible time-travel mission that threatens the existence of this planet. Do you know anything about it?"

The alien watcher tells Ambush that the Eastern Alliance is working with the Antiknock to achieve global supremacy. The Antiknock are an extraterrestrial species with the ability to change their appearance. They crave human blood the way humans crave illegal drugs, and in exchange for the Antiknock's help, the Eastern Alliance has agreed to provide an unlimited supply of humans for the Antiknock's blood-consumption needs.

The alien watcher explains that the hybrid cloning project has grown at a staggering rate. They are moving on to phase 2, spreading hybrid humans throughout Earth's general population. The Grays, a powerful but peaceful extraterrestrial species aligned with the SGOPT, now have hybrid humans in positions of power around the globe, Talbert H. W. Ambush being one of them.

The AB-negative blood type did not originate on planet Earth. The Grays genetically engineered it to eradicate all other human DNA with recessive blood types on the planet. This process occurs when a hybrid human's DNA combines with the DNA of other humans who do not have AB blood type, usually through sexual activity or blood transfusions.

When fire ants come in contact with other species of ants, they completely eradicate those other species. The same happens when hybrid humans with AB-negative blood engage in sexual activity with humans with recessive blood types; they replace the humans' DNA with AB-negative blood.

The Grays plan to create a new dawn on planet Earth, including elevation above level 0 existence: the birth of a civilization having no disease; no discord toward one another; complete unity with one another; no more wars;

a crime-free society; universal health of body, spirit, and mind; use of both the left and right hemispheres of the human brain; complete harmony with the vibration of planet Earth; genuine love for one another; activation of the subconscious mind; and connection with the spirit of the higher self.

Unknown to humanity, these extraterrestrial beings are the architects of humankind's belief system and law structure. The Grays are doing this in order to prevent this level 0 civilization from collapsing into chaos and destroying Earth, which would deny the Grays access to Earth's water resources.

Ambush asks the alien watcher if he knows the identity of the foreign agent tasked with the mission to prevent the assassination of JFK. Zendora lets out an unusual laugh and addresses Ambush by his hybrid name, O'mare, meaning "shining sun."

The extraterrestrial tells Ambush the Antiknock have given their human hosts advanced technology for destructive reasons, because the Antiknock hold nothing but contempt for humankind. The extraterrestrial also tells the T-3D operative the sponsoring nation is in the North Korea.

The most intriguing aspect about the situation is the foreign agent himself is a hybrid human but does not know it. This will prove to be a challenge for Ambush and the unit to deal with.

According to the alien watcher, should the unit fail to prevent history from being tampered with, the Eastern Alliance won't be the real threat to Earth; the war between the Grays and the Antiknock for control of the planet will be.

The boat has traveled a great distance out to sea, and Zendora shuts off the engine. Suddenly the water begins to bubble and erupt around the boat, and then an alien spacecraft breaks the surface of the water to hover above the boat. A hologram bridge extends to the boat. Zendora bids goodbye to Ambush as he enters the UAP, which then submerges to leagues under the sea, where no human has gone before.

JACK MARTINBURG

In September 1963, Tony Hunter, a.k.a. the White Dragon, arrives in the Big Easy with official identification credentials as FBI Agent Jack Martinburg. The real Jack Martinburg has been kidnapped by TTRU snatch operatives and taken to a safe house, which, unknown to the kidnapped federal agent, is an alien spacecraft. He will be held there until the Antiknock can secure him.

Hunter has taken on the facial identity, voice patterns, and mannerisms of the federal agent using the facial-cloning-analysis processor on his T-3D, giving the White Dragon the power of a federal agent and enabling him to track and monitor Lee Harvey Oswald in his efforts to stop him from assassinating JFK.

During an earlier altercation, the man code-named the White Dragon beat down a fellow federal agent named Guy Bannister. In a drunken stupor, Bannister tried to pistol-whip Hunter, thinking he was Agent Martinburg. During his mission brief back in the mountains of China, Hunter was made fully aware that Agent Gus Bannister would be a problem. During the 1960s KGB spies identified him as an FBI agent working for both the Soviets and the CIA. Hunter knows this character can do anything to anyone without provocation. Bannister is also Oswald's handler/coordinator. The double-agent traitor is tasked with providing Hunter, who is posing as Jack Martinburg, with the means to groom, prep, and set up Oswald to take the fall as the lone gunman in the assassination plot against JFK.

Unknown to Bannister, it's Hunter's mission to throw a monkey wrench into the assassination plot and prevent the assassination of JFK. The first item on Hunter's agenda is to pay a visit to Lee Harvey Oswald's residence in Dallas, Texas, to question his wife, Maria-Ann Oswald, the niece of a KGB colonel, to learn the whereabouts of her husband.

Outside Lee Harvey Oswald residence, 604 Elizabeth Street, Hunter, posing as Agent Martinburg, knocks on the front door. To his surprise, Maria-Anna Oswald isn't the one who answers the door; it's Oswald himself, and he knows why Agent Martinburg is at his residence.

"I was beginning to wonder if I had to come and find you, Jack."

Lee motions for the FBI agent imposter to come inside and make himself comfortable.

Hunter is still at a loss for words, now face-to-face with the man who is historically labeled as the man who assassinated the thirty-fifth president of the United States.

"What makes you think I would not come to see you, Lee?"

Oswald peeks out the front curtains.

"Ah, forget about it. Can I get you something to drink?"

Hunter shrugs at the lone gunman's question. "Yeah, sure. Whatever you have is fine with me."

Shortly, Lee returns with two drinks. "What did that fat-mouth Bannister have to say?"

Hunter tells Lee they won't be sticking to the original itinerary, because Bannister told him possible counter surveillance activities are suspected of being conducted on the original plans, which could compromise the Big Dance, as the assassination plot is code-named.

Lee is picking up weird vibes from Hunter, who is impersonating Agent Martinburg.

"For some strange reason I don't feel so peachy about you, Jack."

Hunter's heart begins to pound in his chest.

"What are you talking about, Lee?"

Oswald is now glaring at Hunter, a.k.a. the White Dragon. "I can't put my finger on it. You're just giving me a weird feeling, and I don't like it."

After giving the FBI imposter his drink, Oswald's slowly walks around Hunter. "I'm going to ask you a couple of question, if you don't mind?"

Jack responds with Hunter's trademark smile. "Ask me anything you want if it will put your paranoia at ease so we can get down to business, Lee."

Lee is a CIA agent who managed to convince the Soviets he had defected from America because of his political beliefs. Oswald's places his drink on a small end table next to his chair and then brandishes a loaded handgun, pointing it at the FBI imposter.

Hunter is beside himself with rage, but he doesn't dare let Oswald's know his true emotions, if he wants to live.

"Tell me which federal agency Gus Bannister works for, the FBI or the CIA?"

Agent Martinburg removes his hat, brushes it off, and then places it on his right knee. "He works for both agencies, Lee."

Oswald's smirks slightly. "What position does my wife's father hold in the Soviet Union?"

Agent Martinburg smiles before responding to Oswald's question. "He's a colonel in the GRU/KGB."

Lee Oswald rubs his thigh with the butt of his handgun, being sure to keep the barrel pointed at the man posing as Jack Martinburg. "What secret program did I work on when I was in the Marine Corps?"

Hunter smiles and shakes his head at Oswald's interrogation session. "Really, Lee, you were assigned to the U-2 spy-plane program. Still having strange vibes, asshole?"

Lee waves his pistol back and forth at the man he has no idea is from the future. "I am not done with you yet, Jack. When I was living in Russia, I went by a nickname. Tell me what that name was, Jack."

Lee slowly raises the pistol in the direction of the phony federal agent, ready to shoot him dead if he doesn't know the answer.

Hunter chuckles to himself. "Really, Lee. Your nickname was Alex J. Hidell."

Lee gets to his feet and places the pistol in the waistband of his pants. "No hard feelings, Jack. It's nothing personal, just business. One can never be too careful when it comes to the business of planning the assassination of a sitting president. You understand, don't you, Jack?"

Hunter grabs his hat and places it on his head.

"No hard feelings, but that will be the first and last time you get away with pointing a loaded gun at me, ass hole."

Lee grins at the imposter.

Hunter takes a drink to calm his nerves, realizing that he could have been a dead man in the past, never to have a future if he hadn't done his homework on Oswald personal history.

"Now answer some question for me, Lee. Who wants to assassinate the president and why?"

The Ex-Marine turned CIA double agent goes on to tell the federal agent imposter that the assassination of JFK is for a variety of reasons. The president has begun issuing debt-free US currency[47] and recently rejected Operation Northwoods.[48] He has been accused of betraying the Constitution, encouraging Communist-inspired race riots,[49] illegally invading the sovereign state of Mississippi,[50]

---

[47] The inscription on the back reads, "New money, to replace Federal Reserve notes."

[48] In 1962 the Joint Chiefs of Staff presented Kennedy this operation to authorize our government the right to perpetrate terrorist attacks upon US citizens and blame it on our enemies to justify wars and political assassinations; his response was to seek to dismantle the CIA and its ability to conduct covert operations.

[49] He has been accused of turning the sovereignty of the US to the Communist-controlled United Nations. Enemies of JFK charge him with betraying the United States' friends Cuba, Katanga, and Portugal. On the other hand, JFK has also been accused of befriending the United States' enemies Russia, Yugoslavia, and Poland.

[50] This accusation stems from when the president deployed federal agents to supersede local authorities.

consistently appointing anti-Christians to federal offices,[51] and secretly signing National Security Memorandum 263.[52]

This president doesn't have any strings attached to his administration; he alone is in control. Lee ends his explanation by stating he has no problem participating in the assassination of this sitting president, because the ex–US marine and now CIA clandestine service operative wants to enact vengeance upon the president for abandoning a lot of his good friends, who were involved in the CIA's Bay of Pigs operation, to rot in a Cuban prison.

---

[51] This action creates a Supreme Court with anti-Christian rulings.

[52] This memorandum enables a recall of one thousand American advisers from Vietnam by December 25, 1963; the remainder of the US military will be withdrawn by 1965; SGOPT wants to prevent this from ever happening, at all costs.

ALEX J. HIDELL

L ee tells Hunter the president has made many enemies who want to see his demise. Oswald believes that the conspirators truly think the president has committed treason in their eyes. However, he also believes the assassination is driven by the conspirators' greed and lust for money and power.

Hunter attempts to take advantage of the moment to psychologically discourage Lee from participating in the assassination of the president. It's a shot in the dark, but it's worth a try. Hunter asks Lee if he's ever felt that maybe he might be the scapegoat taking the blame in this assassination plot. Lee tells the FBI imposter it's not his job to think; he's a hired gun, a shooter, an assassin, a messenger boy, nothing more.

Lee fancies himself a history buff, so he tells Hunter that in 1865 President Abraham Lincoln was assassinated, strangely enough, for the same reasons these Ivy League, secret society, organized crime motherfuckers want to kill the current president. Like Lincoln, JFK has upset the balance of power in the government, which is run like a corporation. Like a corporation, when the chief executive officer rocks the boat, the corporate board members fire him. In this scenario, the corporate board members are shadowy figures that fire the chief executive by blowing his goddamn head off.

Lee goes on to explain he's nothing more than an employee, following orders issued by the board-member criminals in high political places. "In their pursuit of the same fucking thing, money and power, this conspiracy goes all the way up to the highest levels of power, my friend."

Lee tells Hunter he's not the only shooter involved in the plot. This revelation shocks Hunter to his core; if what Oswald has revealed is true, that will complicate things for him in accomplishing his mission successfully.

In present-day America, Ambush and Slay prepare to travel back in time to protect the past. Both T-3U operatives are injected with bio-micro-communicators. The receiver is injected behind the ear with a special hypodermic needle, and the microphone device is injected at the base of the thumb muscle. All the user has to do to communicate is speak into the base of the thumb area.

The communication transmission frequency is totally secure from interception; only individuals with the bio-micro-communicators will be able to receive and send transmissions. This system is powered by the electrical impulse of the human body; it never needs to be charged. T-3D support agents have transported back to year 1963 to locate and secure the major figures Ambush and Slay will impersonate to enable them to accomplish their counter–time mission.

The first target to be snatched by time-travel-technology

snatch agents (T-3SAs) is James J. R owley. The current sitting chief of the Secret Service, Talbert H. W. Ambush, will be disguised as him. The second target is E. Howard Hunt, a CIA operative suspected of having taken the fatal shot from the infamous grassy knoll that kills JFK; Ronnie Slay will be disguised as this individual.

These major figures are crucial in the planning phase of the assassination plot; impersonating J. Rowley will enable Ambush to control one of the most sophisticated law enforcement agencies that existed in 1963. He will move in the circle of the assassination conspirators to learn Lee Harvey Oswald timeline and ensure the enemy time-travel agent isn't successful in stopping the assassination of the thirty-fifth president.

The facial features, voice patterns, and mannerisms of Rowley and Hunt are uploaded; both Ambush and Slay are fitted with solid gram masks, and the facial-cloning-analysis procedure provides them with their disguises.

After receiving their final intel briefing, both T-3U operatives are deployed to their assigned sectors in 1963, until they can link up to defend the past.

CAMELOT REVISITED

Outside a public park in Washington, DC, a bright light in the shape of a door appears. Talbert H. W. Ambush steps out from the future into the past in October 1963. The door of light disappears in the blink of an eye. Now disguised as J. Rowley, the T-3D veteran strolls through Rock Creek Park, enjoying the cool evening breeze. He thinks, *My God, the oxygen here is so fresh. I've been breathing polluted oxygen for so long I forgot how fresh air feels.*

Ambush understands that oxygen in the future is very toxic because humans become reckless and destructive, slowly committing global genocide. That's why the extraterrestrials view humans as parasites sucking the planet dry, like a leech sucks the life from a host.

The Secret Service imposter sees a pay phone and stops to call the Secret Service field office to arrange for a ride to J. Rowley home. Ambush has no idea where J. Rowley home is, but he soon finds out after the Secret Service detail drops him off there. J. Rowley residence will serve as the forward base of operations for Ambush and Slays' counter–time mission.

Ambush heads to the study, where J. Rowley is known to keep a secure line. He checks the messages on the classified tape-based Code-a-Phone model 500 answering machine and discovers he is to attend an emergency meeting with some of the assassination-plot conspirators.

In Miami, Florida, a bright light in the form of a door appears in an alley behind a grocery store. A figure steps out of the future into the past. The bright light vanishes in the twinkle of an eye.

Slay, now disguised as E. Howard Hunt, quickly moves behind a Dumpster. He takes this moment to make a radio check with Ambush.

"Secret Chief, this is Phantom Shooter. Copy?"

Ambush responds immediately. "Lima Charlie."

Slay gives his sitrep in short order; he informs Ambush that he is now in Florida and on his way to contact Hunt's partner to learn where he is to meet with him to begin his mission to stop the reversal of JFK's assassination.

"Will update you when I learn something. Copy?"

Ambush is admiring J. Rowley's art collection in his study as he listens to Slays' sitrep.

"Roger. I will do the same."

Before ending the communication with Slay, Rowley reminds the T-3U rookie that it's imperative that he is the primary shooter at the Big Dance.

Hunt crosses the street and strolls down the sidewalk. He learns that people in 1963 are more interested in orbiting astronauts, James Bond movies, and Elvis, who drives teen girls crazy by gyrating his hips on stage during his concerts, than the policies coming out of Washington, DC. In the

Lone Star State, right-wing extremists create a volatile atmosphere before JFK's visits to the City of Hate.

Hunt enters a diner to use the pay phone to call Frank S turgis, the shooter on the grassy knoll during the JFK assassination.

Slay hears a heavy-toned voice through the phone receiver.

"Where are you? I've been looking for you for hours." S turgis takes a slow drag on his cigarette before continuing.

I was beginning to think you got pinched by the feds or something. Lucky for you I didn't call the farmers to report a possible security breech, asshole!"

Right off the bat, Slay realizes that S turgis is an asshole of a guy; he will have to maintain his bearing in order not to blow his cover.

"You should know better than that, partner. I had some unfinished business to take care of before we head to the farm."

"Wonderful. Can we get down to fucking business now? Meet me tomorrow at the usual place, and don't be freak' in late!"

Slay presses his lips together so as not to snap on S turgis and draw unwanted attention to himself.

"Just make sure you're there, my friend."

Frank S turgis meets the man he thinks is Hunt early in the morning and hands him the classified badge he will need once they arrive in Langley, Virginia.

Hours later, the two CIA operatives are dropped off at an undisclosed location in Langley, Virginia, for target practice. They receive a briefing from range instructors, Bay of Pigs veterans who will also participate in the Big Dance. The instructors are members of the highly classified CIA squad known as the dirty tricks team (DTT). Hardened specialists from the clandestine service, DTTs deploy around the world to assassinate world leaders the SGOPT feels are threats to their interests. DTTs also deploy to foreign countries of interest to find ways to undermine those countries' governments and then cause civil war. The SGOPT secretly exploits these countries, causing mass death and destruction. The SGOPT replaces the assassinated leaders with puppet regimes under SGOPT control so that they can rape the target counties for their natural resources.

Their strategy has worked without interference, for the most part, until JFK comes to power. The president doesn't play well with others and becomes a big problem for the SGOPT, which has been terrorizing the planet for decades. The SGOPT marks the president for death because he won't cooperate with their immoral plans. They decide they will forcibly remove him from office, initiating a coup d'état on his administration, at the same time stripping the American people of their constitutional rights, liberties, and freedoms established so many centuries before by the architects of the Constitution.

Somewhere outside Langley, Virginia, Slay and Frank S turgis take turns firing modified M14 sniper rifles. Their targets are mannequins in a moving duplicate of the presidential limousine. The mock vehicle travels at the same speed the actual presidential limousine will be traveling through Dealey Plaza on November 22, 1963. Frank S turgis struggles to connect kill shots on the mannequin where the president will be seated; instead he hits the mannequin sitting where the governor of California is expected to be seated. His other attempts hit the Secret Service driver mannequin, which would be a disaster, to say the least. His next shots hit the mannequin where the First Lady will be seated. After receiving advice from DTT instructors, S turgis aim improves.

On the other hand, Hunt's first attempt hits the mannequin where the commander in chief will be seated in the back of the neck; his second attempt strikes the center of the back of the head of the mannequin representing the president, instantly exploding the dummy's head to pieces. Frank can't believe his eyes. The last time they were at the range, Hunt couldn't hit the ass end of an elephant from twenty-five meters. All of a sudden, now he can't miss. Frank is suspicious about why his partner is suddenly an incredible sharpshooter.

Soon the sniper practice stops for a lunch break. Frank begins to grill Hunt about his new marksman skills.

"Say, buddy, how in the hell did you go from can't hit shit to can't miss shit?"

Slay grins to himself to avoid letting S turgis get under his skin. "I've been practicing with a good buddy of mine who happens to be a marine scout sniper instructor."

S turgis launches a huge ball of chewing tobacco spit on the ground, barely missing Slay.

"Oh yeah? What's your buddy's name?"

Slay continues to eat the lunch provided for him by the firing-range instructors.

"Now why would I give up the names of my contacts to you? Do I ask you about your personal assets?"

S turgis glares at the man posing as E. Hunt.

"What's the big fucking deal, Eddie? Just give up this

Marine's name." Frank flicks the non-filter cigarette but on the ground before speaking

"Maybe I want to get some private sniper lessons too." S turgis grins, exposing his tobacco-stained teeth.

"Look, Frank, just drop the subject, I'm not giving up my connect to you or anybody else, alright."

Hunt stares S turgis down.

Both men are asked to return to sniper practice.

UNITED SNAKES

I nside a ballroom at the exclusive Stork Club in New York City, the conspirators plotting the demise of the thirty-fifth president gather. Ambush finds himself in the company of the who's who in the highest circles of government, news media, and organized crime connected to the SGOPT. This meeting was called to discuss the last details of the assassination plot, which must succeed without fail, including who will do what. Should damage control be needed once the assassination is initiated, the news media is told to be prepared to use news broadcasts to distribute propaganda and keep the general public in a state of confusion.

SGOPT members will be on standby. Secret Service agents, should the president manage to survive the assassination attempt, will ensure the president dies, at all costs.

Ambush is at a loss for words as he hears how well detailed their plan to eliminate JFK is, but he must stay in character so as not to draw suspicion to himself and become an unsolved homicide, never to be heard from again.

"Gentlemen, I have taken care of the tasks requested of

me," J. Edgar St. Hoover says. "I trust the rest of you have done the same."

Everyone in the ballroom bursts out laughing at Hoover's sarcasm.

The rest of the guests confirm they too have done their parts so the assassination plot will proceed without interference from outside authorities. The SGOPT have invested hundreds of millions of dollars in Southeast Asia and will be damned if they will stand by and allow JFK to ruin their international business plans.

It is now becoming clear to Ambush why these wealthy pigs really want to take out a sitting president. It has nothing to do with JFK committing treason and all that jazz; these scumbags simply want to take advantage of third world markets and become wealthier.

During this time, America was known as the "Great Society." In 1963, the push-button telephone was introduced, first-class postage stamps cost five cents, and nearly sixteen thousand military troops were deployed to Southeast Asia to fight an invisible enemy, faced with trying to achieve victory in an unwinnable war the American people didn't want anything to do with.

Outside on a New Orleans street, Lee Oswald speaks out against America's oppression of Cuba. He hands out Communist leaflets supporting Castro. Hunter stands in the shadows observing Oswald from afar; he can't help but wonder why Lee can't see he's being set up to take the blame for the assassination plot against JFK. The FBI imposter badly wants to tell Oswald that his future holds nothing but death and ridicule. That could spark the decline of him wanting to follow through with attempting to kill the president, but Hunter knows Oswald, consumed with love and patriotism for his country, will do whatever his puppet masters ask of him. Oswald was conditioned as a marine to immediately obey orders.

After verbally spouting support for Communist Cuba, Lee Harvey Oswald completes his duties. He has passed out most of the Communist leaflets he received from a Cuban secret police agent masquerading as a dishwasher in a local restaurant.

Next, Hunter has Lee Harvey Oswald pose for a picture, holding the last of the Communist propaganda materials along with an M1 rifle, which will later be used as disinformation to frame him as the lone gunman in the assassination plot against the president.

Agent Bannister instructed Hunter to have Lee do this task. The rookie TTRU operative doesn't dare deviate from his duties; he wants to maintain his cover and, most importantly, stop the assassination of JFK. So Hunter simply tells Oswald the photo is going to be used by pro-Cuba activists living in Miami for recruitment purposes.

Ambush and the other conspirators leave the Stork Club after they complete the final details of the assassination plot. Ambush is dropped off at the New York International Airport.[53] Unlike the general public, who fly on crowded commercial airliners for an uncomfortable flight, Ambush boards a private jet provided by the government, occupied only by him and the pilot. Ambush is on his way to

---

[53] JFK International Airport didn't exist in 1963.

Washington, DC, to attend an important meeting at the Treasury Department.

After the jet climbs to a comfortable flight pattern, a bright light appears inside the cabin. Ambush isn't the least bit surprised. The T-3U vet simply enters the portal and finds Zendora, the alien monitor, waiting inside for him.

And then Ambush finds himself in the middle of the mysterious, remote, classified extension of Edwards Air Force Base known as Area 51.[54] Zendora has transported himself and Ambush to the top-secret base to pass on vital information pertaining to the assassination plot.

---

[54] Actual name is Area 51, a.k.a. Dreamland, where alien spacecraft and bodies are believed to be housed.

HYBRID-HUMANOID CONNECTION

"Why have you brought me here, Zendora?"

The alien monitor teleports both to another period placing Slay and his alien monitor inside the cockpit of a stealth bomber, located in an authorized-only aircraft hangar.

"To fill you in on the complicated situation that brought about the demise of a great soul."

"I hate when you just show up out of the blue, Zendora."

The aliens monitor responds to Ambush's complaint with his strange laughter. "Yes, I understand, O'mare. This is Area 51 as you know; it's one of the most secure places on planet Earth. I can speak openly with you here, without fear of being overhead by the wrong humans."

The extraterrestrial tells Ambush that Area 51 was created by the first officials of the SGOPT, along with his fellow Grays as decoys, in order to deceive and draw in all suspicious and nosey UFO interest groups and prevent them from discovering the actual experimental aircraft base, which is underground somewhere in the state of Colorado. Zendora gets down to the business of explaining the true motives surrounding the assassination of JFK.

"It starts with recovering a spacecraft in 1941, a few days after Pearl Harbor is bombed. Secretly, government officials started collaborating with extraterrestrials in 1942.

"And then, as you know, a shadow group of government officials recovered another spacecraft later in the desert during the Roswell incident. This also led to collaboration between government officials and extraterrestrials. JFK became aware of this unsanctioned relationship between humans and extraterrestrials. Once he found out that these extraterrestrials were providing the military elite with advanced technology in exchange for Earth's water resources, the president became outraged and demanded accountability of how this could happen under his administration.

"This situation alarmed the president because he was concerned that, should the Soviets get wind of this, it could cause them to launch a nuclear strike against the West as an act of self-preservation. So JFK decided he would go public with the proof that extraterrestrials were alive and well on Earth, collaborating with government officials. This outraged SGOPT officials associated with the space program, who went on to create the climate that led to the conspiracy to silence the president."

"All the rhetoric that has been published in history books all these decades has been nothing more than disinformation to keep the masses in a state of confusion.

"The president was killed because he was going public about officials connected to the SGOPT since the '40s being in a working relationship with extraterrestrials, such as myself and others that have come to this planet for decades."

The alien watcher explains how the body of unsanctioned officials views the president's actions as a threat to US national security and how an investigation of this magnitude would lead to the discovery that human DNA engineering has been going on for some time in the United States and that has led to the creation of a hybrid-humanoid species. In addition, the United States' covert time-travel operations would be exposed.

To reveal that government officials have been kidnapped and held hostage on alien spacecraft and that T-3U operatives have been impersonating them on foreign soil, committing espionage and all types of other international crimes with impunity, would be a huge disaster for the US government.

"Those buffoons you've been in the company of are conveniently in place to cause confusion and provide conspiracy theories for the public to consume for years to come. By the time all the theories and conspiracies are decades old, the public won't give a damn who assassinated JFK.

"In other words, you now know the truth about why this great leader was killed, so there won't be any doubt creeping into your mind when the time is right. Let Ronnie Slay know the truth that has been revealed to you. You must succeed on this mission, to protect the past, for your species and mine."

"That's fucking incredible, Zendora. You have my word—we won't fail. We can't afford to."

The extraterrestrial and the hybrid humanoid bid one another goodbye. Talbert H. W. Ambush, disguised as J. Rowley, activates his T-3D, returning him to America, 1963.

Slay and Frank S turgis sit inside a train boxcar, en route to Dallas, Texas, to infiltrate Dealey Plaza. It's a textbook CIA strategic mode of transportation. The two CIA operatives are disguised as hoboes to avoid drawing attention to themselves while they conduct their reconnaissance and locate the best sniper nest. For security purposes they take turns sleeping, as they have weapons and ammunition two hoboes would have no business transporting.

Slay, who Frank Surges thinks is E. Howard Hunt, can't help feeling uneasy about what lies ahead of him. He especially wrestles with the fact he will be the shooter who ends the life of the thirty-fifth president.

Slays' thoughts drift to a moment back in Fort Benning on the pickup day he and the other recruits met their Ranger instructors.

"Reveille!"

Ranger instructors (RIs) assault the recruits while they are fast asleep in their beds. "Get your sorry asses out of the rack!"

Several of the RIs snatch recruits from their racks, mattress and all, slamming them hard to the floor.

"Move it, move it!"

Ronnie Slay is frozen with fear; he can't react fast enough. He finds himself being snatched out of his rack and thrown to the floor by a wild-eyed RI who is wearing a black T-shirt, a large black-and-gold Ranger tab spread across the front of it. On his head is a patrol cap with his rank insignia below a small black-and-gold Ranger tab.

"Get your slow ass up, you lazy pup! Move it, move it!"

Slay doesn't know if he should be excited or afraid that the first day of Ranger School has finally arrived. Slay stands next to his rack, watching in amazement the controlled chaos the RIs are inflicting on the confused and disoriented recruits. Slay's moment of observation is interrupted when an RI snatches him by the back of the neck and forces him down in the direction of his ruck.[55]

"You want to join the rest of us sometime today, or do you need a fucking invite?"

Slay can't believe how powerful the Ranger is. The second lieutenant literally feels like a newborn baby in the grip of the army commando instructor.

"Sorry! I'm not sure what it is you want me to do!" Second Lieutenant Slay shouts.

The RI leans down, putting his face next to Slay's before responding. "Pack your shit and get your ass outside with the rest of the fucking pups!"

With that, the Airborne Ranger pushes Slay onto his ruck and storms off to launch another attack on an unsuspecting Ranger recruit. Amid all the chaos, the only thing that keeps running through Slays' mind is why the RI keeps referring to him and the rest of his fellow recruits as *pups*.

After packing his belongings in a hurry, Slay makes it outside to join the rest of the other terrified recruits in formation.

Slays' train of thought is interrupted when as Frank S turgis wakes up from his nap.

"What time is it?"

Slay quickly composes himself.

"Half an hour past the time you were supposed to be up."

Surges wipes moisture from both eyes. "Why in the fuck didn't you wake me up then?"

---

[55] Military term for a backpack.

Slay lets out a huge yawn. "Forget about it. I couldn't sleep if I wanted to."

Surges removes a pack of cigarettes from his breast pocket.

"What's the matter, Hunt? The fact that you're the primary[56] fucking with you?"

Slay stares down at the boxcar floor.

"Naw, it doesn't bother me one bit to assassinate our president, because he wants to do the right thing for our country, Frank."

Frank Surges laughs hysterically. "Right for fucking who? He's ruining this country faster than it took to build it!"

Surges lights his unfiltered cigarette and takes a long drag. "Hell, he's giving the country away to the Communist-backed niggers, supporting their bullshit civil rights movement so they can destroy the country us white folk worked so hard to build."

Slay can't believe S turgis attitude, but it dawns on him he is in 1963 America.

"This country is just as much theirs as it is ours."

This time, Surges takes a quick drag on his cigarette. "This can't be E. Howard Hunt talking like a fucking Communist, the same guy who kills jigaboos to discourage them from voting."

S turgis points his cigarette in the direction of the man he thinks is E. Howard Hunt.

"Let me refresh your fucking memory, pal. It was you who shot an uppity jigaboos in the balls because he had the nerve to dare cast his vote during public elections."

---

[56] The main shooter on the sniper team.

Slay is now coming to understand that if Hunt did what Frank S turgis claims he allegedly did to another human being for trying to exercise his constitutional right to vote, the man he is posing as is a total psychopath. Instead of getting upset, Slay remains calm.

"That was then; this is now."

"Wow, so you're a nigger lover now Hunt?"

Slay slowly gets to his feet as Frank S turgis approaches him in an aggressive manner, getting too close for Slays' comfort.

"What's your fucking point, Frank?"

S turgis flicks his cigarette to the box car floor, and then grinds it out with his right foot.

"My fucking point is, now that niggers aren't slaves, they are just taking up space in our country, Hunt."

Slay grins in Frank S turgis face, because Agent Slay has had enough of S turgis mouth.

"You sound like a stupid, pissed-off redneck, Frank."

Frank S turgis attempts to invade Slays arm space, by walking up on him in a hostile manner, which Slay views as a threat. He removes a dagger from its sheath, holding it out to the side so Frank S turgis can see the blade.

"If you feel foggy, then jump, S turgis, because I'll gut you like the pig you are, and won't lose any sleep after doing it.

"I can complete this mission without your dumb ass."

"I'll just tell Langley you couldn't stomach doing the mission and went AWOL somewhere, never to be heard from again."

THE ETERNAL FLAME
IS NOT LIT

C hills run down Frank's back, because He doesn't recognize the gaze coming from behind the eyes of the man he believes is E. Howard Hunt. S turgis backs down very slowly, keeping his eye on the blade in Slays' hand.

"Stay cool, Eddie, don't do anything stupid." S turgis goes in his shirt pocket to remove the pack of non-filter cigarettes, and lights another.

We both need to stay focused on accomplishing this mission—what do you say?"

The T-3U rookie operative returns the dagger to its sheath.

"Let's do that."

The only sound heard now is the click-clacking of the train's magnets rolling across the tracks.

The official flag of the Treasury Department is displayed for the first time in 1963. Ambush, who is posing as the chief of the Secret Service, walks past cast-iron columns in the money-management agency to attend a secret meeting. Also in attendance are members of the SGOPT, along with several representatives of the owners of the Federal Reserve Bank.[57]

The agenda of the meeting is how to get rid of the president, because he's arrogant enough to dare to remove Federal Reserve notes, to replace them with United States notes.

On April 5, 1933, Franklin D. Roosevelt, by design, drafts and signs Executive Order 6102, forbidding the hoarding of gold and silver in America. He issues the executive order to force Americans to exchange any gold or silver in their possession for the newly established Federal Reserve notes.

Federal Reserve notes become the new world currency for the purchase of services and goods, leading the United States down the path to becoming a debtor nation. The financial scam perpetrated on the American people happens not only in the United States but all over the globe.

In 1963, JFK wants to rain on the banking scheme because it's nothing more than legalized extortion of the general public, as far as he is concerned.

The banking elite, white-collar criminals, view the general populous as sheeple who are too stupid, in their opinion, to figure out this global banking scam. The banking officials explain to the man they believe to be J. Rowley that, as the chief of the Secret Service, he is to immediately give the order for the Treasury Department to stop printing US notes and then reinstate the printing of Federal Reserve notes once the president is declared dead.

---

[57] The Federal Reserve Bank is believed to be owned by the Rothschilds and the Bank of England.

Unknown to the president's antagonists, his motivation behind printing US notes is to bribe the American people in order to gain their loyalty, similar to Julius Caesar, who did the same in ancient Rome to win over the Roman mob. JFK's plan is to win a second term in the White House; his ultimate goal is to set himself up as the first king of America. His administration isn't called Camelot for nothing.

In the sky over Louisiana, Lee and Hunter are relaxing in a commercial jetliner, headed back to Dallas. It's October, and final plans are being organized for the Big Dance. Hunter takes another stab at trying to pick Lee Harvey Oswald's brain and learn more about the other shooters involved in the plot against the president.

"Lee, let me in on the secret."

Lee sheepishly turns his head in the direction of the imposter posing as Jack Martinburg.

"What secret would that be, Jack?"

Hunter leans toward the aisle and speaks in a low tone of voice.

"This would be about the other shooters involved in the Big Dance next month."

Lee grins sarcastically. "I'm the only shooter, Jack. I'm the one who's going to knock his dick in the dirt."

Jack is not buying the arrogant assassin's answer and decides to attempt another approach. He is briefly interrupted when a stewardess shows up to ask if either of them would like something to drink. They both decline.

"What's the problem, Lee? Don't you trust me, buddy? I am your case officer, for crying out loud."

Oswald smirks at Hunter's annoying behavior.

"It's not a matter of me trusting you, Jack. It's just that Gus doesn't trust you not to get drunk off your ass and start shooting your mouth off about the show, you understand, don't you pal?"

Jack realizes he isn't going to get any information out of Lee, so he drops the subject, before Lee starts to get suspicious.

"Can you at least tell me if you know of any good diddy bars[58] we can check out when we get to Dallas?"

Lee's eyes widen when he hears the words *diddy bars.*

"You're talking my language now, Jack! Of course I know a great diddy bar, and we don't even have to pay to get in."

"Do tell, how you going to pull that one off, Lee?"

The former Marine turned double agent leans in closer to the aisle, speaking low.

"My good buddy Jack Ruby is the owner of the best diddy bar in Dallas area, that's how."

Jack Ruby is a key figure in the plot against the president. According to the classified KGB files Hunter received in his debrief intel report, Ruby is a midlevel associate for organized crime; he is also the guy the mob goes to for access to unsavory characters to do licks[59] for the mob in the city of Dallas.

Hunter will capitalize on this situation to try to catch Lee in a moment of weakness and pick his brain for more intel on the assassination plot.

Lee and Hunter settle in their hotel room. Lee contacts

---

[58] Slang in 1963 for stripper bars.
[59] Slang in 1963 for committing crimes.

Jack Ruby. Later that evening he and the imposter posing as Jack Martinburg arrive at the most popular nightclub in the city of Dallas, Texas. They are met by one of Jack Rugby's girls, who takes them out of the line straight into the club.

GHOST WARRIORS'

Hunter and Lee are escorted to the VIP lounge. Normally, only the rich and famous get this treatment, pampered and entertained by some of the prettiest and sexiest women in Dallas. No restrictions are enforced in the lounge.

Shortly, Jack Ruby makes his way into the VIP lounge to ensure Lee and his guest are being well taken care of.

"Lee, you cocksucker!"

How the hell you been?"

The club owner gives Lee a bear hug, lifting him off his feet. Lee's manhood is being compromised, so he quickly puts a stop to the embarrassment.

"Put me down, you big schmuck." After being let go by Ruby, Oswald introduces his guest.

"Come over here. I want to introduce you to an associate of mine."

"Jack, meet Jack," Oswald says in a sarcastic manner. He chuckles out loud.

Lee tells the club owner that Jack Martinburg is a friend of a friend, street talk to inform mob-connected associates that a person isn't a snitch or a law enforcement problem.

Jack Ruby sizes up Lee's guest, to which Ruby has no idea is really an imposter posing as an FBI agent.

The club owner tells a couple of his employees to make sure Lee and his friend get anything they want, on the house.

As the night goes on, Lee enjoys the company of sexy and beautiful women. He consumes bottle after bottle of liquor, until his judgment is impaired.

Lee grabs a handful of a hostess's ass as she walks by. He nearly falls on his face when he tries to pursue another sexy hostess, who is shaking her ass in a seductive manner in front of the drunken double agent.

Hunter prevents Oswald from smashing his face against the wall when the woman pushes him away from her.

"Hold your horses, Lee. Can't have you injuring yourself before the Big Dance, now can we?"

Jack takes Lee to an unoccupied booth in the corner of the VIP room; this is where the FBI imposter will grill Lee for intel about the Big Dance.

Meanwhile, after leaving the VIP room, Jack Ruby contacts an organized crime boss conspirator in Chicago from his office phone to update the mob boss on the situation in Dallas.

"Boss, guess who finally showed up. Yeah, that sack of shit doesn't have a clue what's really going on."

"He's got some guy with him. He says he's a friend of ours."

Jack Ruby uses a key to open a secure drawer; removing a lockbox. Ruby dumps a pile of money from the lockbox on the top his desk and begins to count stacks of fifty- and hundred-dollar bills. The mob connected business owner continues to listen to the crime boss on the other end of the phone. Ruby ensures the mob boss that everything is still in play for November.

"I never seen this guy before, if you ask me, he looks like he's keeping a close eye on the little schmuck."

The club owner puts a stack of bills in a counting machine as he chuckles to himself.

"This guy looks like one of J. Edgar Hoover's guys. Yeah, boss, I know. The little schmuck is stupid, but I seriously don't think he's suicidal, because that's what he will have to do if I find out he brought the feds to my joint."

Rugby can be heard laughing it up with the crime boss through his office door, which is cracked open.

"Lee won't be around much longer after the Big Dance, believe me."

The midlevel organized crime associate tells the crime boss he is having Lee's friend checked out as they speak, to ensure he's not a threat to their plans against the president.

While in a drunken stupor, Lee begins tell Hunter that two other assassin squads will be in Dealey Plaza next month for the dance.

This confession shocks the rookie TTRU operative; his heart pounds in his chest. Now he knows there truly will be other shooters involved in the assassination of the president. This will make it much tougher to accomplish his mission to stop the assassination of JFK. Hunter thinks, *How on earth can I possibly stop more than one shooter? I can't be in more than one freak 'in place at the same time.*

Hunter is contemplating contacting his superiors to have them dispatch additional TTRU assets to help him accomplish his mission for his Eastern Alliance comrades. Hunter understands failing to accomplish this mission will mark him as a traitor. He will be executed for bringing shame upon them.

Hunter presses Lee for more information about where the other shooters will be in Dealey Plaza. Even though Lee is drunk and belligerent, he's aware of what Hunter is trying to get him to do, and he won't cooperate.

Lee tells Hunter he has no idea who or where the other shooters will be next month. He tells Hunter to contact his boss in Washington, DC, if he wants more information on the other shooters, and then he walks off to harass more sexy hostesses.

Hunter dismisses contacting his Eastern Alliance superiors, as it will be viewed as a sign of weakness. Instead, he comes up with a plan to disarm Lee. He will use Lee's weapon to locate and take out the other shooters.

SHAPE-SHIFTER BLOODLINE

Inside a private government office, the man posing as J. Rowley contacts Hunt.

Slay, still on the train to Dallas, moves slowly to the far side of the boxcar to avoid waking the sleeping Frank S turgis.

"Phantom Shooter, this is Secret Chief."

Slay responds quietly,

"Send your traffic, Secret Chief."

As Ambush speaks to Slay, he looks out at the huge white clouds surrounding the aircraft speeding toward California.

"What's your status, Phantom Shooter?"

Slay speaks quietly into the base of his thumb, keeping an eye on S turgis to be sure he doesn't wake from his slumber.

"I'm en route to the area of operations with Foxtrot Sierra."

Frank S turgis shifts and changes his sleeping position, continuing to snore as he does so.

Slay continues his sitrep. Ambush then informs Slay that he will arrive in Dealey Plaza after a quick meeting in California to provide fire support for Slay and Foxtrot Sierra.

Ambush was notified at the last minute to attend an eleventh hour meeting, called by the conspirators of the plot against JFK.

The meeting is to be held at a secret society club by the name of the Coconut Grove in California.

The Secret Service imposter was told it's a tradition to anoint their schemes with protection against failure. Unknown to Ambush, the extremely wealthy and powerful people gathering at this exclusive country club are actually coming together to perform a satanic ritual to receive blessings from Baphomet, whom these members believe to be a high-ranking demon. They pray to Baphomet for protection against their enemies. Rumor has it that the members lure unsuspecting people as guests of honor with the promise to show them a good time, when in fact they intend to sacrifice these individuals to Baphomet, part of the ceremony to gain favor from the demon. Members believe that power is released to this demon when it consumes the blood of the unsuspecting people duped into attending this ceremony of death.

These immoral individuals have been deceived to believe they are dealing with demons, when in all actuality these are extraterrestrials hostile towards humanity.

These particular extraterrestrials can shape-shift into any form; these aliens choose to take the shape of bloodthirsty demons so they can openly gorge on human flesh and blood.

These extraterrestrials came to Earth millions of years ago to excavate precious metals for various needs on their planet. The shape-shifters decided to create a race of slaves to do the hard labor for them; these extraterrestrials began experimenting and were successful in grafting a humanoid race of slave workers by conducting human-DNA-engineering experiments. A lot of the DNA experiments weren't quite successful; several mutant humanoid fiascoes were created during this period of DNA engineering, producing creatures making up most of ancient Greek mythology: Cyclops,[60] centaurs,[61] Leviathan,[62] goliaths,[63] sirens,[64] Medusa,[65] Empusa,[66] Gorgons,[67] Harpies,[68] Lamia,[69] the Graeae,[70] satyrs,[71] the Sphinx,[72] and Typhon.[73]

After a while, these extraterrestrials were successful in engineering a DNA map that enabled them to create a hybrid-humanoid race of slaves that went on to become modern humans. These hybrid humans labored in the earth to excavate precious metals that these extraterrestrials lust for.

---

[60] Giant one-eyed monsters that feed on humans.
[61] Half-man, half-horse creatures.
[62] A sea creature.
[63] Thirty-six-foot-tall giants.
[64] Sea creatures that drive men to suicide with their bewitching song.
[65] Monster with snakes for hair.
[66] Creature that feeds on the blood of men.
[67] Sisters of Medusa.
[68] Half-woman, half-python creatures that feed on small children.
[69] Creature that melts the skin of anyone who looks into its eyes.
[70] Creature that sips the blood from its victims.
[71] Hybrid humans known for pleasure and passion that lead to their partners' deaths.
[72] Creature that asks people a riddle and devours them if they can't answer correctly.
[73] Creature that has a human body and is said to be taller than a mountain.

Eventually, the hybrids launched a rebellion against their extraterrestrial creators, intending to eradicate the aliens' species, but they weren't successful in completely defeating their alien masters. The damage inflicted on the excavation site was more than the extraterrestrials cared to deal with, so they took all the precious metal they could carry aboard their spacecrafts and left planet Earth for their home planet, known as Planet X. These extraterrestrials swore to return, to reclaim Earth as their property and re-enslave the hybrids they'd genetically engineered.

Several thousand years later, the extraterrestrials returned to planet Earth and began interbreeding with human women, giving way to a cross race of hybrid humanoids, an extraterrestrial species known as shape-shifters. These extraterrestrials have gained and maintained a pure bloodline.

LANCER

These extraterrestrials have a foothold of power and entitlement in every nation on Earth. When they find humans with their DNA bloodline, those alien humanoids are made aware of their extraterrestrial birthright and are brought into the fold of privilege and prestige. It's the nature of these alien beings to ensure their offspring are well taken care of throughout their lives, wanting for nothing.

It has been documented in rare situation where humans were able to record activities, displaying a shape-shifter humanoid becoming excited and then morphing into its true form, a reptile- or a lizard-like humanoid species.

Humans can't see shape-shifters' true forms, because the Earth's vibration is three-dimensional; the shape-shifters' vibrational signal derives from their galaxy in the fourth dimension, thus giving these extraterrestrials the power of physical cloaking.

The government jet carrying Ambush touches down in Northern California; he gets into a limousine that is waiting to whisk the imposter posing as the chief of the Secret Service to the secret society club, the Coconut Grove.

Suddenly, Ambush receives a call on the limousine phone. It turns out to be J. Edgar Hoover, wanting to thank him for coming to the last-minute meeting. This gathering is made up of rich and powerful people connected to the SGOPT from the elite political, corporate, and military sectors. Hoover tells Ambush that he invited him to make up for all the lost time between them.

The limousine pulls up to a huge black steel gate that automatically opens. The Secret Service imposter compares the moment to the gates of hell being opened. Once the limousine is inside the compound, a very attractive, scantily dressed young woman approaches the vehicle. She opens the limousine door for Ambush.

"Welcome back to the Grove, Mr. Rowley"

Ambush is taken by surprise by how extremely friendly the young woman is being to the man he is posing as.

"Excuse me—how do you know me?" Ambush is lost for words. He has no idea who this woman is, so he just stands in place, staring at her large, firm breasts.

"I can't believe you don't remember me, Mr. Rowley."

She giggles; her breasts move in sync with her quiet laugh.

"It will come back to you who I am."

Ambush blows her comments off as the odd ranting of a young woman wanting attention. Ambush tells the young woman to enjoy the rest of her day. At the same time she squeezes her arms together, causing her large, firm breasts to bulge and give Ambush some eye candy.

She then asks Ambush what he would like for his entertainment pleasure later, after the festivities: a young female companion, such as herself; two young women, such as herself plus another hostess; or one or more young boys for his bedtime pleasure?

Ambush is caught completely off guard; he asks the hostess whether this is sick joke, and she assures him that this is protocol, the very protocol he is credited with implementing.

The hostess begins to flirt with the man impersonating J. Rowley, asking if he would feel better if she used the words "for your sexual entertainment" instead of "bedtime pleasure," and then she smiles.

The hostess goes on to tell Ambush she knows he'd prefer a woman such as herself to screw his brains out, because last time he was there, they had sex all night long. Then she inquires if that jogs his memory. Eventually, Ambush asks the hostess for her name, which she says is Bambi.

She explains he chose her on his last visit to the Grove because J. Edgar said she was a virgin waiting to have her cherry popped. She lets out a seductive laugh; once again, she presses her breasts together for the enjoyment of the man she believes to be J. Rowley. For a second time the sexy hostess propositions Ambush about what he would like for his bedtime pleasure. Ambush tells her he will get back in touch with her later, as of now, he needs to hurry and attend the festivities.

She appears disappointed that he doesn't choose her on the spot. She was looking forward to enjoying another long period of perverted sex with him. What better way to celebrate her seventeenth birthday?

Ambush heads to the area where the festivities are scheduled to be held, thinking, *What in the world is going on at this place, where high-level government officials are having sex with minors?*

Finally, Ambush meets a Grove staffer, who tells him that he is late for, and cannot participate in, the run-and-hunt games. The escort takes him to the room where he will be staying at the Grove.

Everything in the Grove is big, both in size and display. There's a personal bar stocked up to the teeth with the best liquor money can buy, fitted with a king-size bed with a mirror above it. Ambush can't help but think of the young hostess when he spots the mirror above the bed.

Shortly, Ambush is taken to a supply room, where he is given a hooded black robe and is told to place it over his clothes; it is required to attend the festivities. Ambush acts as if he already knows what the staffer is talking about and knows what to expect at these festivities.

Ambush finds himself standing in front of a huge stage with a giant owl, with huge glowing eyes, on it. The members chose the owl as their mystical symbol because owls can see in the dark. They compare this trait with their ability to see in the dark of wisdom. Members believe the owl to be a fierce hunter; they believe this trait mirrors their ability to hunt victims for their human-sacrifice ceremonies to the demon Baphomet. Members compare their victims to rodents, which the owls hunt in the dark, striking with no mercy on their prey.

Ambush is led to his seat near the ritual stage, along with several other members wearing hooded black robes. Some of the participants' hoods are down, revealing their identities. Ambush recognizes several of the participants as high-level political personalities in the government. There are also high-level law enforcement officials and celebrities in attendance.

A loud bell sounds; a voice comes across an intercom system instructing all members to place their black hoods over their heads and stand in front of the ritual stage.

Several members wearing hooded black robes come into view, escorting two badly injured people. A pair of other members escort another injured person onto the stage. The members secure their badly injured subjects onto three posts that stand upon the ritual stage.

The members exit from the stage to take their places on the floor below. There are three victims on the stage now, two men and one woman. They are all bleeding from injuries sustained during the run-and-hunt games.

Some type of accelerant fluid is thrown on a pile of wood in a pit area to the right of the stage, and the pile is set ablaze.

MASS CORRUPTION

Two individuals in hooded black robes exit the stage; the members on the floor below the stage begin to chant in a chorus. The lights dim as four members in hooded black robes appear on the stage and begin to dance in a frenzy.

Without warning, they disrobe, exposing their nudity. The two couples begin to dance around the three injured subjects tied to the posts on stage.

Ambush is shocked and thinks this is just a harmless, ridiculous ritual, but he couldn't be more mistaken. Talbert H. W. Ambush is about to witness human sacrifices to Baphomet. The members desire to receive Baphomet's blessing for a successful assassination plot against the president without any interference.

These rituals have been going on since SGOPT elitists collaborated with bloodthirsty extraterrestrials. A shapeshifter humanoid is able to deceive the elitist Grove members to believe it is a powerful demon that craves human flesh and blood for its pleasure and that is to be worshiped. It will bless anyone who fulfills its desires for human blood because the consumption of human flesh and blood gives these extraterrestrial humanoids a high that is equivalent to the high cocaine gives human beings.

Flesh and blood is also highly addictive to these extraterrestrials, just as cocaine is highly addictive to humans.

The four members dancing in the nude begin having sex on stage directly behind the three badly injured subjects tied to the posts. The injured victims are going into shock from the wounds they sustained during the games. Suddenly, a very tall, huge figure walks out onto the stage, dressed in a hooded black robe like the rest of the Grove members.

As the members on the floor begin to chant loudly, like a chorus, the very tall subject disrobes, displaying a huge, stiff erection. The creature, whom Grove members believe to be Baphomet, has the anatomy of a two-legged centaur, with hideous fangs, hooves, and two horns sticking out of its forehead.

Now the creature begins to dance around the three injured victims tied to the posts, and then it proceeds to engage in sex with one of the male members behind the badly injured victims. After having its fill of sex with the nude Grove member, the extraterrestrial goes on to attack the first victim tied to the first post. It plunges its fangs into the man's neck, mauling him to death.

A staffer now removes the restraints from the dead man, picks the man up over its head, and tosses him into the bonfire. The beast attacks the second man, again plunging its fangs into the victim's throat, mauling him to death. This time one of the nude female members on the stage cuts into the dying man's chest and removes his heart. She and her nude male partner take turns licking the blood off the human muscle as Grove members increase the tempo of their wicked chant.

After the extraterrestrial tosses the second dead body into the bonfire, the nude female member on the stage hands the human heart to the huge creature. The beast devours the human tissue like it's a tasty snack. One of the nude Grove members on the stage cuts the last badly injured victim loose.

All four members begin to engage in a sexual orgy with one another as the beast engages in sex with the injured female victim. The beast plunges its fangs into her jugular vein, sucking and draining her blood supply until she's dead.

The creature grabs the dead woman by her neck and throws her lifeless body into the bonfire. The Grove members in front of the ritual stage slow their wicked chant; eventually the song of death ends.

After the beast gets its fill of sex, flesh, and blood, it exits the stage just as quickly as it appeared. The four nude Grove members toss their hooded black robes into the bonfire and follow.

No longer in a state of shock, Ambush realizes he has just witnessed a shape-shifter massacring three people. Most disturbing of all, the T-3U agent, along with the other Coconut Grove members, has been complicit, involved in three homicides. Ambush knows his hands are tied in this crime. If he chooses to take action, he risks affecting the course of history.

His train of thought is interrupted when he is accosted by J. Edgar St. Hoover.

"James, how good it is to see you again. I thought you stood me up when I didn't see you here for the game."

Ambush thinks, *I'm disgusted by what I witnessed here today, and this sick son of a bitch is trying to flirt with me.*

Ambush can't afford to show his true feelings and risk blowing his cover. "I apologize, Edgar. My flight was delayed for some strange reason, but I made it here as fast as I could. I wouldn't have missed this for the world, my friend."

It's extremely difficult for Ambush not to laugh out loud at how the head of the FBI acts like a lovesick schoolgirl. Ambush tries to ignore J. Edgar St. Hoover's flirtatious behavior.

"Good. Is there any possibility we could spend the rest of the evening in each other's company, James?"

The head of the FBI bats his eyes at the special agent from the future, precisely the situation Ambush was hoping to avoid.

Just in the nick of time, Ambush spots J. Edgar Hoover's full-time lover, Clyde, mean-mugging them both. Clyde appears to be suspicious and more jealous by the minute; his lover is spending too much time in Ambush's company.

J. Edgar Hoover must have felt a hole being burned in the back of his head. He turns around to see Clyde speed-walking in his direction.

He quickly tells the man he thinks is J. Rowley how nice it was to see him again; he wishes the chief of the Secret Service good luck in his future endeavors and tells him not to be a stranger.

Clyde and Edgar walk away, bickering like two uptight women. Ambush grins at the spectacle as he watches the two men argue. Ambush thinks, *Don't worry, Edgar. My future awaits me in another era, where you won't be able to trouble me ever again. Good riddance.*

Ambush heads back to his room to clear his mind of the horrific events he witnessed in this wicked place. He enters his room and is shocked to find the sexy young hostess in his bed.

"What the hell are you doing here?"

The sexy hostess sits up in the king-size bed, revealing that she is wearing a very seductive red-black-and-white negligee.

"Don't be mad at me, James. You never got back to me about who you wanted for your bedtime pleasure, sweetie."

TRIANGULAR KILL ZONE

The T-3U agent has a good mind to tell the sexy hostess to get the hell out of his room, but after the stress of the mind-blowing day he has experienced, Ambush decides he's glad the sexy hostess is in his bed. He lets her stay because he needs to release some tension.

Without reservation, Ambush engages in all-night sex with the young hostess. He is a hybrid humanoid; in his mind, he's doing his part to help elevate planet Earth above a level 0 civilization consciousness. Plus, Talbert H. W. Ambush can't help himself, because he is now influenced by the mannerisms of J. Rowley.

Somewhere on the outskirts of Dallas, Texas, on November 21, 1963, Ronnie Slay, posing as E. Howard Hunt, and Frank S turgis arrive in a commuter train boxcar at the train yard near Dealey Plaza.

About forty-five minutes later, the train prepares to enter Dealey Plaza's train hub to be inspected for repairs for the next three days. The stage is set for the two assassins to infiltrate Dealey Plaza and find the best place for their sniper position for the Big Dance tomorrow.

Slay and Frank S turgis blend in with other hobo transits

to avoid possible detection by the ever-watchful eye of the Secret Service's advance-party agents. They split up so that if one of them is detained by authorities, the other will be able to continue to scout for a good sniper position.

Later that day, after scouting the entire presidential route Lancer[74] is expected to travel, Slay and Surges carefully make their way back to the boxcar to compare notes and discuss the best location to set up their sniper position.

Surges explains to Slay that the first solo shooter will be positioned in the Texas School Book Depository building; the second team of shooters will be set up perpendicular to the book depository. Slay and Surges agree that their sniper position needs to be set up in such a manner to create a triangular kill zone, ensuring that JFK will have no chance of survival as his limousine travels through Dealey Plaza.

Surges informs Slay that there are secret elements in place to ensure JFK is set up for failure during the operation. For instance, the First Lady, who has had enough of JFK's cheating ways, especially his filthy affairs with Marilyn Monroe, will convince the president to ride with the limousine's bulletproof top down.

After the shooting starts, certain Dallas motorcycle police officers will watch for anyone in the crowd taking pictures and report them to the feds. The FBI will target and confiscate those citizens' cameras in the name of a federal investigation.

Slay and S turgis conclude that the best position for their sniper position is the grassy knoll on the final stretch of the

---

[74] Secret Service code name in 1963 for JFK.

presidential motorcade route. There, Slay will have a straight sight line to take his shot. A shooter couldn't hope for a better sight alignment.

Plus, the grassy knoll is adjacent to the train hub, where the boxcar currently sits, providing Slay and Surges with an excellent displacement route. After assassinating Lancer, they will be able to discard their sniper equipment and weapons in the hidden compartment in the boxcar floor.

Elsewhere in Dallas, Oswald and the man posing as federal agent J. Martinburg are in their hotel room, sleeping off another night of hard partying at Jack Rugby's club; actually, Oswald did most of the partying for both.

Hunter isn't able to sleep. The issue of other shooters being involved in the assassination plot is weighing heavily on the TTRU rookie's mind. This is a very big problem for him and will make it difficult for him to be able to prevent the assassination of JFK. Hunter knows if the assassination isn't prevented, he won't be able to return to the future without being executed by the Eastern Alliance for failing to accomplish his mission.

On November 22, 1963, Talbert H. W. Ambush is inside a government jet, speeding toward the major city of Dallas, Texas, from California. The T-3U agent will be in position to provide fire support for Ronnie Slay, ensuring that the assassination is a success.

The private jet carrying Ambush touches down at Dallas International Airport, where a limousine is standing by to take the phony Secret Service chief to Dealey Plaza, where he will set up his command post to provide fire support for Slay. Ambush receives constant reports of Lancer's movements on a police scanner. He hears that Lancer has just landed at Dallas International Airport and is en route to Dealey Plaza; the commander in chief's ETA is forty-five minutes. Ambush contacts Slay via his bio-micro-communicator and tells him to get into position ASAP and stand by for the arrival of Lancer in forty-five mikes.[75]

Slay passes the information on to Frank S turgis.

"How the hell do you know that? I didn't hear any radio traffic."

Slay quickly opens the hidden compartment in the boxcar floor.

"Don't worry about that, asshole. I just have a hunch. Do you want to debate how I know this intel, or do you want to help me get into position to take the freak 'in shot?"

Oswald is now in position inside the book depository; the CIA double agent has a police scanner too, enabling him to monitor the radio traffic of the Dallas police department and receive real-time intelligence about the president's movements, allowing the lone gunman to keep track of the president's movements until he reaches his line of sight.

---

[75] Military slang for minutes.

Relight the Eternal Flame

After a while, the presidential motorcade comes into sight three blocks away from Dealey Plaza. As soon as Oswald hears the motorcade is three blocks from Dealey Plaza, he makes his way to the sixth floor of the book-depository building and secures his sniper rifle outfitted with a scope.

There's a bolt-action rifle next to him, a decoy to fool the authorities that will flood the sixth floor after the president is assassinated. The sniper rifle Oswald will use to shot the president is made of hard clay. After Oswald uses the specialized weapon, he will smash it to bits and then place the trigger group, barrel group, bolt group, and firing pin on his person until he can discard them where they will never be found as evidence. He heads to his egress route to the movie theater to meet the SERE (survival, evasion, resistance, and escape) contact assigned to him by the CIA.

The time has come for Oswald to exact payback from the man holding the highest office in the land. Lee Harvey Oswald thinks, *Mr. President, you left so many of my buddies to die in a Cuban prison on an operation you and your fucking brother hastily threw together in an attempt to make your self-centered ass look powerful at the expense of the lives of brave men who faithfully served this country for decades. Not to mention that your arrogance nearly plunged the world into a nuclear holocaust because you had the audacity to make a life-or-death decision for the entire country. Guess what, Mr. President—today I decide it's you who will die.*

The presidential limousine makes a left into Dealey Plaza, below and in front of Lee Harvey Oswald's sniper position. The Ex-Marine turned CIA double agent inhales and slowly exhales as he squeezes the trigger on his sniper rifle, keeping his scope crosshairs focused on the top of the president's head. He fires.

At the same time, Oswald receives a punch to the right side of his face, altering the path of the bullet. The shot strikes Lancer in the back of his neck. Immediately the president grabs his throat; he's unable to yell for help, because his voice box is damaged from the full-metal-jacket round that passed through his throat.

On the sixth floor in the book depository, Oswald recovers from the punch delivered to his right jaw. To his shock, Oswald discovers the devastating punch came from the man he believes to be Jack Martinburg, who is now standing over him, holding Oswald sniper rifle at port arms[76].

Oswald shakes off the daze from being punched.

"I knew there was something odd about you. Who the fuck are you! Secret Service?"

Hunter continues to stand over Oswald at port arms.

---

[76] Military neutral stance with a weapon at chest level

"Where are the other shooters, you sorry sack of shit?" Hunter places the barrel of the weapon on Oswald's groin area before addressing the assassin.

I'm going to shoot you in the balls first, then your knees, and finally your fucking face if you don't tell me what I want to know, now!"

Lee Harvey Oswald chuckles at the TTRU rookie's threats, and then he slams his right shin into the specially made sniper rifle, shattering it into bits, leaving the man posing as Jack Martinburg holding only the barrel and stock of the sniper rifle.

Below, on Dealey Plaza, Slay looks through the scope of his sniper rifle down his sector of fire, as snipers are taught to do. Slay scans his sector of fire from nine o'clock, twelve o'clock, three o'clock, and six o'clock and observes a ruckus unfolding on the sixth floor of the book-depository building between Hunter posing as Jack Martinburg and Lee Harvey Oswald.

Slay watches Hunter's attempts to smash Oswald in the head with what appears to be the barrel of a rifle. But Oswald manages to avoid the strike and pulls a handgun on Hunter. To Slays' amazement, as he watches the two subjects fight, the man posing as Jack Martinburg displays the trademark smile of his best friend. Slays' moment of distraction is interrupted by Frank S turgis.

"Hey, Hunt, you with me here? Lancer is in range. Take the fucking shot!"

Slay returns his focus to the task at hand.

"Relax; I'm with you." Slay looks through the sniper

scope and picks up his target, the president of the United States.

"Just waiting for a clear shot. The First Lady is too close to Lancer for me to take the shot right now, Frank."

S turgis quickly uses his binoculars to verify Slays' claim.

"Roger. You better not let this son of a bitch get away, Lancer is only wounded right now."

Lee Harvey Oswald first shot only gave the president a flesh wound. His full-metal-jacket round went through the president's neck and hit the governor of California, coming to rest in the governor's left thigh, causing the governor to panic and shout, "They're going to kill us all!"

The second sniper team, made up of members of the CIA's dirty tricks team, opens fire on Lancer, grazing the president on the left side of his skull and slamming him against the First Lady, who also panics. "Get him off me! I don't want to die!" She pushes JFK away from her.

On the sixth floor of the book depository, Oswald turns the tables on Hunter, shoving his handgun in the FBI impersonator's stomach. Oswald doesn't pull the trigger, because he doesn't want to draw attention the sixth floor should there be authorities in the building.

"You're too late. The other shooters are firing on the president. Guess what—they're better shots than I am."

Oswald slowly backs away from the man posing as Jack Martinburg.

"Now I'm going down the steps, and you're going to remain here, Jack, so you can watch the other snipers blow your beloved president's fucking head off, whoever you are, motherfucker!"

Oswald rushes down the stair case of the book depository. He is careful to check that there are no cops storming the place. He makes it to the sidewalk outside of the building and comes face-to-face with Talbert H. W. Ambush, who is posing as J. Rowley.

"Good afternoon, Mr. Hidell. Don't worry; the Big Dance will be a successful operation, I promise you that, my double agent friend."

For a moment, Oswald dumb founded, shocked, trying to figure out who this strange person is, who knows his Soviet cover name. Lee Harvey Oswald thinks to himself; *this is the CIA's way of letting me know I'm being set up to take the fall for killing the president?*

"Who the fuck are you?" Oswald brandishes his 22 caliber snub nose pistol at the posing as J. Rowley. Agent Ambush doesn't flinch at all at the sight of Oswald brandishing his pistol in his direction.

"How do you know my cover name? I'm not going to let you CIA pricks set me up."

Ambush leans against the book depository and chuckles. What Ambush would really like to do is shoot Oswald dead, but he'll settle for mind-fucking him, which won't alter the future.

"History tells me that you've been set up as the patsy for the assassination of JFK from the start, my friend. You better get out of here while you can, Alex —or do you prefer Lee?"

Impostor posing as the chief of the Secret Service grabs Oswald by his shirt collar, jerking the lone gunman close to his face. Lee is too shook to try to use his handgun on the stranger; he can't afford to blow his chance to make his escape and link up with his SERE contact.

"Oh, by the way, tell your wife, M aria-Anna I said hello."

And then Ambush pushes Oswald to the away from him by muzzling him in the face. The scapegoat assassin quickly runs away from the book-depository building as fast as his legs will carry him.

After running for some distance, Oswald is approached by a Dallas police officer by the name;

J.D. Tippit. Oswald thinks the cop is a CIA operative in disguise sent to kill him; without hesitation, Lee Harvey Oswald shoots the cop four times, killing him instantly.

Back at Dealey Plaza, the moment of truth is at hand; Frank Sturgis tells the shooter he thinks is E. Howard Hunt that the First Lady is now clear of the target. Slay slowly squeezes the trigger on his weapon, sending a 7.62 full-metal-jacket round downrange and striking Lancer in the forehead, blowing his brain matter all over the back of the presidential limousine.

The First Lady becomes so terrified after watching her husband's brains being blown all over the back of the limousine, she tries to jump off the back of the limousine. A Secret Service agent from the chase car following the presidential limousine prevents her from doing so.

As soon as the First Lady is secured inside the limousine, the Secret Service driver punches the gas pedal, speeding in the direction of Parklawn Memorial Hospital.

Right away, Slay and Frank Sturgis return to the boxcar under the cover of confusion and chaos erupting around the streets of Dealey Plaza. After entering the boxcar, Slay and Frank Sturgis systematically place all their equipment and the sniper rifle in the secret compartment in the floor of the boxcar.

Authorities scramble to the book-depository building they believe to be the location where the sniper fired shots at the President of the United States.

Several cops make entry into the building; Ambush identifies himself as the chief of the US Secret Service. He directs the frantic police officers toward the upper floors of the building.

The police conduct a floor-by-floor search. When they arrive on the sixth floor, they discover a bolt-action rifle leaning against a window frame overlooking the route the president's motorcade traveled.

RETURN OF THE
WHITE DRAGON

Currently on the sixth floor of the book depository is an unidentified man posing as FBI agent Jack Martinburg.

"Get your fucking hands up!" Tony Hunter, posing as an FBI Agent.

Tony Hunter does what he is told. One of the cops conducts a hasty frisk of his person and discovers that the un-sub[77] carries FBI credentials.

"Sorry for the misunderstanding, sir, but can you tell us why you're up here on the floor where a sniper is suspected to have taken shots at the president?"

Hunter is devastated. He comes to the realization that he has failed to prevent JFK's assassination. "How is the president?"

The cop is stunned as he watches a tear run down the face of the man posing as a federal agent.

"I'm not sure how the president is. That information is

---

[77] Unknown subject.

being withheld from the public right now. Again, can you explain why you're up here, sir?"

Hunter slowly wipes the tears off his face.

"Yes, I can explain, I am attached to the presidential security detail." Hunt presents the phony documents provided to him by his TTRU chain of command before his mission.

My assignment is classified, so I can't go into detail."

The FBI imposter clears his throat before launching into a bullshit explanation for why he is on the very floor where shots were fired at the thirty-fifth president of the United States.

"I was in the process of investigating this building as a possible location where someone could take a shot at the president. I heard shots ring out. And then I observed a suspicious man flee from this location, running in what direction, I couldn't tell you."

Suddenly radio traffic comes across all the police officers' radios. "Officer down, near the movie theater."

Several cops rush down the stairway and head in the direction of the movie theater. The other police officers continue to search the sixth floor for evidence to confirm that a sniper indeed fired shots from this location at the president.

Before long, Ambush makes his way up the stairs to the sixth floor to observe law enforcement activities unfolding. Upon arriving on the sixth floor, Ambush is overcome by a strong vibe that only another hybrid humanoid would give off. Then he spots an odd person standing among the cops.

Likewise, Hunter also receives a strong vibe. The rookie

TTRU operative turns to observe Ambush, who is posing as the chief of the Secret Service.

"And who might you be, sir?" Ambush asks.

Hunter looks Ambush up and down. "I am Agent Jack Martinburg from the FBI—and you are?"

Ambush realizes that the vibe is extremely strong when he stands next to Hunter. "I am James Rowley the chief of the Secret Service."

Face-to-face with the head of the Secret Service, Hunter becomes uncomfortable. Hunter knows he must choose his words very carefully to avoid drawing suspicion from the man who has failed to protect the president and who can easily confirm or disprove any story Hunter lays on him.

"So how did you end up in the very place where a suspected sniper is alleged to have taken shots at the president?"

In the back of his mind, Ambush thinks, *Could I be standing face-to-face with the enemy agent sent back here to prevent the assassination of JFK?*

Hunter answers, "I have already explained to the police how I came to be on the sixth floor, sir."

Ambush tells Hunter that was the wrong response, especially coming from a federal agent. "Now explain the story again to me. I'm not the police, and I'm not in the mood for your smart-ass attitude. Do we understand one another, Agent Martinburg?"

Hunter becomes defensive after Ambush's verbal assault. "As a matter of protocol, show me some form of identification, if you don't mind."

After the man provides his credentials, Hunter tells the

Secret Service imposter that he is attached to the presidential security detail on a classified basis.

"On what basis might that be, Agent Martinburg?"

Hunter explains to Ambush that he was dispatched to Dallas based on threats the president received from the area. His boss felt that enhanced security was needed for the presidential detail and needed to be on a classified basis, to prevent would-be adversaries from becoming aware of the enhanced presidential security.

Ambush finds Hunter's story suspect. Agent Martinburg's boss is one of the main conspirators involved in the plot against the president, so to Ambush, the story comes across as false. Since Ambush is posing as J. Rowley, though, he won't let the man he believes to be an FBI agent know of his suspicion.

"I'll have you know, your boss and I are great friends."

"So, I don't know why he didn't inform me about this matter of enhancing the president's security."

Hunter displays his trademark smile, Ambush is overcome with enormous feeling of Deja' vu about this guy, but Ambush can't put his finger on why.

"As I stated before, it's because the assignment is classified, sir."

Ambush's mind is working on overdrive. Why does he feel he's had an encountered with this guy before?

"You remind me of someone—I just can't put my finger on it."

Ambush removes a small note book from his suitcoat pocket.

"But it will come to me; I'm sure of it."

Ambush's comment spooks Hunter, and he now goes

into escape mode to keep from blowing his cover by the Secret Service chief, who unknown to Hunter is also an impostor from the future.

"If there isn't anything else you need to know from me, you will have to excuse me."

"I have to be heading out to help with the aftermath from the president being assassinate, you do understand, don't you?" Ambush can't stop the FBI Agent or whoever he is, from leaving, so Ambush relents.

"I will be giving your boss a call to confirm your story about being on a classified assignment here in Dallas." Ambush waves his hand at the phony fed to leave.

"You're free to go."

The T-3D Vet smirks as Tony Hunter aka the white Dragon makes his escape by the skin of his teeth.

Without delay, the man posing as Jack Martinburg makes his exit from the book depository, brushing against the Secret Service chief as he does so. Tony thinks to himself;

'Call whoever the hell you want to call, asshole. By tomorrow I'll be transporting back to the future, after I devise a new plan to redeem myself in the eyes of the Eastern Alliance.'

Among the panic and chaos still erupting on the Dallas streets of Dealey Plaza, police officers eventually stumble upon Slay and Frank Sturgis hiding spot.

"Hey, what are you two bums doing in this boxcar?"

Agent Slay thinks quick on his feet, because he notices that Sturgis is slowly removing a pistol from his ankle holster.

Slay and Sturgis maintain their cover by staying in character, as Slay weights in.

"Fuck you! Who the hell are you calling a bum!"

The cop doesn't get angry; he figures the two hoboes are drunk, and that's why they are being belligerent with him. The police officer uses a little patient as he takes charge of the situation.

"All right, you two need to come out here right now."

Sturgis, who is sitting close to Slay, gives the T-3D rookie a slight elbow to single he is going to take the cop out. Slay slowly shakes his head, signifying don't do it.

The cop is momentarily distracted by a fellow cop telling him to wrap it up so they can transport everyone in custody to the police station.

Slay takes this opportunity to quickly hide his T-3D, and Sturgis weapon under some hay just in front of the hidden floor panel. And then, the cop returns his attention back to what he thinks are two hobos.

"Didn't you two bozos hear all the gunfire out here earlier?" the cop asks.

Slay and Sturgis start laughing out loud together. Slay replies.

"Yeah, we thought it was the Fourth of July or something."

Now the cop begins to laugh out loud with the assassins in disguise.

"It's November, you idiot." The cop moves in to lend a hand to who he thinks are two drunks.

"The president has just been shot, and everyone in the vicinity is being rounded up for questioning, so get your asses out here now!" Both CIA shooters cooperate with no phony objections, as Sturgis says;

"Oh, come on, man. I just got a fresh bottle of Mad Dog to suck down."

"Do we look like we're in any fucking condition to hold a fucking gun, let alone to fucking fire one?"

The cop laughs again at the antics of the two hoboes as he physically removes the men from the boxcar to take them into custody for questioning. He places them in the back of a police paddy wagon to be transported to the Dallas police headquarters where they will remain until the investigation of the shooting of JFK is fulfilled.

Hunter, disguised as Jack Martinburg, sits in a local bar, watching the news report about the condition of the president. He learns the commander in chief is said to be in critical condition but still alive. Hunter thinks that maybe he still has a chance for redemption, because if the president survives, the Secret Service will tighten security, making another assassination attempt nearly impossible. Tony Hunter, a.k.a. the White Dragon, will return to the future as a revered hero after global power belongs to the Eastern Alliance.

The news report switches to a scene showing LBJ, along with the First Lady, surrounded by several government figures. LBJ is being sworn in as the next president of the United States. Now the situation hits home with Hunter like a ton of bricks; even if the president doesn't die, he won't be serving as the commander in chief, so the future will be left in favor of America maintaining its grip on global power.

Hunter comes to an understanding that if he returns to the future, he will be signing his own death warrant.

Instead, Hunter contemplates staying in the past; since he's a federal agent, he could live a life of entitlement. Hunter could portray himself as a law enforcement prodigy. Being from the future, he will have firsthand knowledge of future happenings and will be able to predict and prevent serious events before they happen, including the assassination plot against RFK, the Tet Offensive in Vietnam, the assassination attempt on MLK, criminal activities of terrorist groups like the Weathermen, serial killers like the Zodiac Killer, the Manson Family murders, the terrorist attack at the Berlin Olympic Games, the assassination attempt on President Richard Nixon, the kidnapping of Patty Hearst, and so forth and so on.

These achievements by Hunter would go down in history, making him the greatest FBI agent to have ever served in the Federal Bureau of Investigation—possibly even the greatest FBI director ever to have run the most sophisticated law enforcement agency in the world.

THE LOSS OF AMERICA'S INNOCENCE

Inside a holding cell in a Dallas police station, Slay, Frank Sturgis, and the rest of the hoboes rounded up earlier in Dealey Plaza are waiting to be questioned by police investigators. A police officer opens the door to the holding cell and takes half of the bums to be questioned. One of them is Frank Surges. The man posing as E. Howard Hunt remains in the holding cell.

Slay uses this window of opportunity to contact Ambush using his bio-micro-communicator. Slay moves to the corner of the cell for the transmission.

"Secret Chief, this is Phantom Shooter. Copy?"

At that moment, Ambush is on a landline speaking with a Secret Service agent for an update on the condition of Lancer. When he receives a signal on his bio-micro-communicator, Ambush tells the special agent to keep him updated on any changes in Lancer's condition.

"This is Secret Chief. What's your status, Phantom Shooter?"

"Secret Chief, I'm currently sitting in a holding cell at the Dallas police station. Copy?"

"Good copy, Phantom Shooter. Am en route to have you released. Copy?"

"Roger."

Before he disconnects, Slay explains that he needs Ambush to go to boxcar 0013 and retrieve his T-3D; he had to hide it there when he was taken into custody by the cops.

"I copy. Boxcar 0013. Over and out."

Ambush packs a government suit for Slay to change into once he is released. Ambush is going to have Slay pose as his driver. They'll go to the hospital together, and Ambush will get the status on Lancer.

Ambush's limo pulls up to the Dallas police station. The man posing as the chief of the Secret Service enters the police station and sees a police detective interrogating Lee Harvey Oswald in an interview room.

"Can I help you, sir?"

Ambush turns his attention to the cop manning the front desk.

"I hope you can. You have a man in custody by the name of E. Howard Hunt. I am here to take custody of him."

The cop asks Ambush to show him some form of identification. He chuckles under his breath.

"Do you find something funny, Sergeant?"

The cop stops laughing immediately when Ambush displays the Secret Service credentials identifying him as chief of the Secret Service.

"As I was saying, you have a man by the name of E. Howard Hunt in your custody, and I want him released to me now. Can you manage that task without losing your professional bearing, Sergeant?"

The cop lowers his head in shame as he heads to his chief's office.

"What can I do for you, Mr. Rowley?" asks the police chief.

"I am here to have a man by the name of E. Howard Hunt released to Secret Service."

The chief of police crosses his arms in front of his chest. "What is the reason for this man to be released into the custody of the Secret Service?"

Ambush presses his lips together in irritation.

"It's classified. The only thing you need to know is that E. Howard Hunt is to be released to the Secret Service without delay. Do we understand one another, Chief?"

The law enforcement official didn't get to be chief of the Dallas police by playing hard-ass with federal law enforcement officials who supersede his authority. So, the Chief of Police authorizes the release of the man he thinks is E. Howard Hunt.

Slay is released from custody at the same time the Dallas police charge Lee Harvey Oswald with the murder of a Dallas police officer.

Ambush can now secure Ronnie Slay, two Dallas detectives come into view escorting Lee Harvey Oswald out the back of the police station as a security measure.

Ambush and Slay decide to follow the police detectives and Lee Harvey Oswald. A crowd of reporters has gathered to capture a picture of the lone gunman accused of shooting the most powerful man in the world.

The detectives almost reach the vehicle that will transport Lee Harvey Oswald to be arraigned in court when suddenly, from out of nowhere, Jack Rugby emerges from the crowd of reporters holding a handgun. As the stunned crowd looks on, along with the entire country watching the incident on live television, Jack Rugby guns down Lee Harvey Oswald.

An ambulance arrives to rush Oswald to the hospital. As soon as the ambulance exits the police garage, Slay suggests to Ambush that this could be a trick by conspirators to help Oswald escape from justice. He recommends they both follow the ambulance to ensure this isn't a CIA recovery tactic to free Oswald.

Both Ambush and Slay hurry to the limousine; the man posing as the chief of the Secret Service tells his assigned driver, "Agent Rogers, take a three-day vacation. That's an order. I have a qualified substitute driver. I'll explain later."

Slay is still dressed in his hobo attire, and the driver gives him a once-over. Ambush realizes this is an odd situation but lets it play out. His driver doesn't put up any resistance, because who is he to disagree with the boss of the Secret Service?

Ambush and Slay head out in hot pursuit of the ambulance carrying Oswald. The two T-3D Agents catch up with the emergency vehicle and cut it off. Both imposters from the future jump out of the limousine and approach the ambulance with weapons drawn. Slay opens the back of the emergency vehicle while Ambush secures the driver.

"What the hell are you doing, mister?"

Ambush grabs the driver by the collar of his work shirt, removing him from the driver's seat.

"Get the fuck out of the vehicle if you value your life."

In the rear of the ambulance, Slay orders the ambulance employee sitting in the back of the emergency vehicle to exit immediately.

AGENT OSWALD, MR. HIDELL

O nce they secure the ambulance, Slay and Ambush speed off in the opposite direction from Parklawn View Hospita l, leaving the two first responders standing in place, dumbfounded over what just happened.

Slay stares at the badly wounded Lee Harvey Oswald. The lone gunman tries to put on a brave face, despite his injuries.

"Who the hell are you? Who sent you, the mob? Is that why that cocksucker Jack Rugby shot me? They don't want to pay me my freak 'in money for doing their dirty work?"

Slay has no doubt that Oswald is mortally wounded; this isn't a CIA trick to help him escape justice.

"No, I'm not from the mob," Slay says. "I'm nobody."

Slay watches Oswald and is overcome with compassion for the marine turned scapegoat. Being from the future, he knows what history has taught him: Oswald was groomed for failure from the outset. The powers that be preyed on his patriotic call to duty to eliminate all threats to America, domestic and foreign, even if that threat happened to be the president of the United States.

Oswald is struggling to catch his breath, and he coughs up blood that runs down his chin and neck.

"Why did you hijack the ambulance? You've been sent to silence me, right?"

Slay shakes his head slowly, answering no to Oswald's paranoia. "Looks like the other guy beat me to the punch, pal. Tell me—what made you think you could shoot the president of the United States and get away with it?"

Slay thinks, *This poor bastard never had a chance. He will forever remain the guy blamed for shooting the president when in fact I'm the one who assassinated him.*

Slay tries his best, but he can't stop his eyes from tearing up, sending tears rolling down his face for Oswald.

For whatever reason, Oswald attempted to assassinate JFK. The T-3D rookie knows why he himself did it: to uphold his oath to defend the past, protect the present, and preserve the future of America and its allies by any means necessary. It doesn't make it any easier for Slay to feel victorious about it.

With the little strength Lee Harvey Oswald has left, he manages to laugh at the man from the future posing as E. Howard Hunt.

"Don't shed a tear for me. You think I'm some lone nut who just wanted to kill the president?"

As Oswald continues to laugh, he spits out blood. Slay has seen Rangers under his command in this condition; Oswald is slowly bleeding to death. But he continues to explain to the T-3D rookie who's who in the conspiracy hierarchy.

"This assassination plot goes up to the highest levels in

politics, law enforcement, organized crime, and military leadership—you have no idea, pal."

The lone gunman coughs up more blood, which then begins to pour out of his mouth. Oswald is drowning on his own fluids. Before he dies, Slay takes time to ask Oswald a question that has been eating at him before Slay pulled the trigger on the president.

"I saw you in the book-depository building with another guy. Why were you fighting with him during the attack on the president?"

Slays' question influences Oswald, as if Slay gave him a shot of adrenaline.

"Oh, that cocksucker, that was Jack. He was supposedly my handler for the assassination of the president, or so I thought."

Oswald's health is rapidly declining, so Slay knows he must try to get answers before he passes.

"Why were you two fighting?"

Oswald breathing becomes labored. "That son of a bitch turned out to be double agent. He tried to stop me from assassinating the president. Go figure."

Oswald statement stuns Slay. It's as if he's been shot by a hollow-point bullet to his forehead. He truly feels the man fighting with Oswald was Tony Hunter.

Finally, the injuries Oswald suffered at the hand of Jack Rugby end his life. Ambush drives the ambulance back to the location where he and Slay left the limousine. To their surprise, the two first responders remained at the same location, still bewildered. Ambush and Slay return the emergency vehicle to them.

"No need to run code. Your passenger is dead. If your

supervisors ask you what happened, tell them it wasn't personal. It was government business."

Ambush tells Slay they need to head to the hospital to wrap up their business.

After Slay changes out of his hobo clothes, both he and Ambush head in the direction of Parklawn View Hospital to confirm they have successfully accomplished their mission.

At the same time, Ambush uploads the facial features of his assigned driver using the facial-cloning procedure so Ronnie Slay can assume the driver's identity.

As Slay drives toward the hospital, he tells Ambush what he learned from the dying Lee Harvey Oswald. The most important fact Slay learned during his conversation with the deceased was the identity of the foreign time-travel agent sent back to prevent the assassination of JFK. Talbert H. W. Ambush's eyebrows rise after hearing Slays' comment.

"Do tell, Who is this foreign agent, Ronnie?"

Slay looks at Ambush in the rearview mirror.

"It's Tony."

Ambush lowers his head in disbelief.

"Why do you refuse to accept that Tony Hunter isn't coming back? Ambush slowly shaking his head as he reasons with Ronnie Slay.

"You really have to let him go, Ronnie."

Slay checks the road and then returns his attention to the rearview mirror.

"Listen—Oswald told me that Tony was posing as an FBI agent."

This statement makes Ambush completely tone in now, because of his earlier encounter with the odd federal agent in Dealey Plaza.

Tony was posing as Oswald's handler; pretending to groom Oswald for the assassination of JFK. Ambush rubs his face at Slays' comment. "He fucking told you it was Tony Hunter?"

Not actually."

Now Ambush is getting irritated. Ronnie Slay adds.

"His cover name was Jack something."

Now Ambush knows Slay is on to something, because Ambush wrote the name of the off federal agent in his notebook during his encounter with the strange FBI character.

I didn't get a last name, because Oswald died before I could, but this Jack character tried to prevent Oswald from killing the president."

Suddenly Ambush recalls named Jack. And blurts it out.

"His name was Jack Martinburg." Ambush replies.

How do you know this Uncle Bush?"

Ambush slams his fist against the door panel.

"Son of a bitch! I knew there was something odd about that guy."

Slay returns his attention to the rearview mirror as Ambush tells him about his encounter, with the person he now believes is Tony Hunter.

"I spoke with an FBI agent in the book depository named Agent Martinburg." Ambush is disgusted.

"I'll fill you in later, about my encounter with Hunter."

Slay takes the final turn toward the hospital where the mortally wounded president lies.

The limousine pulls up to the emergency area of Parklawn View Hospital. Slay exits from the driver's side to open the door for Ambush. The imposters enter the hospital lobby and are immediately approached by Secret Service agents stationed there. The agents stand down once they realize that one of the men entering the emergency lobby is J. Rowley who they believe is their boss.

"Sir, we weren't told that you were coming, or we would have made arrangements for your arrival."

Ambush quickly scans the lobby to see if any members of the press are present and is glad to see that his agents followed protocol by keeping them out.

"I didn't want anyone to know I was on my way. Where have they taken Lancer?"

The agent in charge tells the man he thinks is the chief of the Secret Service to follow him to the operating room where JFK is.

Slay, disguised as Ambush's assigned driver, attempts to accompany him to the emergency room.

"Sorry, sir, you have to remain here," the agent in charge says.

As Ambush's assigned driver, Slay doesn't have the clearance to be near the dying president.

"Sorry, sir," the agent says to Ambush. "We're only following protocol."

Ambush realizes that the agent is doing his job, so he nods to acknowledge he understands where the federal agent is coming from. "Very well. Outstanding job, young man. I will be back shortly."

Ambush stands in the presence of the several select government officials who have gathered to learn the fate of the country's wounded leader. After a while, the chief surgeon approaches the gathering of high-ranking officials to announce that the president of the United States passed away at 1300 hours central standard time from bullet wounds to his head.

The silence in the hospital hall could be cut with a knife.

The imposter posing as the chief of the Secret Service quickly leaves the hallway with a heavy heart and then departs from the hospital with Ronnie Slay posing as his assigned driver.

Many speculate that J. Rowley leaves in haste to avoid being ridiculed by the press for failing to protect the president. In fact, the real reason Ambush makes a hasty exit from the hospital is because he wants to try to locate Hunter, who is posing as Jack Martinburg.

Slay and Ambush get back into the limousine and drive off to an undisclosed location. The two T-3U agents step out of the limousine and enter a bright light in the shape of a door. The bright light transports them back to the future and vanishes as fast as it appeared.

They return to the ultra-secret satellite agency compound located in Seal Beach, Los Alamitos, California, where Talbert H. W. Ambush and Ronnie Slay are congratulated for a job well done. By defending America's past, they prevented a future attack.

Economics, the New Battlefield

B oth agents are debriefed and have their scanned disguises removed. Their bio-micro-communicators are removed from their bodies with specialized extraction equipment.

The two T-3D agents take time to reflect on the events they experienced and survived during their counter–time mission to America in 1963.

"What are we going to do now that we know Tony is alive and well, fighting for the other side?"

Ambush takes a long sip of his gourmet coffee.

"I have a suspicion we haven't heard the last of Tony Hunter, but when he resurfaces, the T-3D will be ready to take him down."

Ronnie Slay thinks to himself;'

Damn right I'll be ready for Tony. And when we do meet, I will give him the chance to explain why he felt he needed to betray his country—before I put a bullet between his eyes.'

One evening in 1963, an alien spacecraft appears in the desert on the outskirts of Dallas, Texas. A bright beam of light shines down from the UAP and then disappears.

The UAP vanishes in the twinkle of an eye. Left

standing on the ground are two individuals who wander aimlessly in the desert: the real James J. Rowley, chief of the Secret Service, and the real E. Howard Hunt, the man who was supposed to fire the shot at JFK on November 22, 1963

Both are returned to Earth after being held in a state of suspended animation on a UAP in support of Big Dance.

Both federal agents will bear the brunt of the blame for the death of the thirty-fifth president, along with Lee Harvey Oswald.

At least, that's how it will be written in the history books, alongside the many other assassination conspiracies.

Elsewhere in Washington, DC, the TTRU operative posing as FBI agent Jack Martinburg is determined to set things right with the Eastern Alliance after failing to prevent the assassination of JFK. Hunter comes up with a plan to redeem himself; he launches a covert operation of his own that will prove to be just as devastating to the United States and its allies as the attempt to stop the assassination of JFK would have been. Under the cover of anonymity in the nation's capital, Hunter uses his federal credentials to gain entry to the US Treasury Department

When the man posing as J. Rowley becomes distracted, Hunter brushes past him and lifts his Treasury access card, during their first encounter in Dealey Plaza.

Hunter makes his way into J. Rowley's office. Once inside, the TTRU rookie uses the access card to open J. Rowley's private safe. Hunter proceeds to help himself to one-hundred-dollar, fifty-dollar, and twenty-dollar press plates.

With these US currency plates, the man posing as an FBI agent is now in position to redeem himself in the eyes of the MSS intelligence agency. With these currency plates, the Eastern Alliance can print as much US currency as desired and flood the global market with American money, causing inflation to rise to the point that the American economy will collapse.

The worst recession America has known since the Great Depression will give the Eastern Alliance the ability to buy America instead of fighting a bloody war against it America.

Present time China- The White Dragon has returned to the future to be de-briefed.

"This plan is brilliant." A senior MSS Agent in Charge says;

"Why spend hundreds of millions of dollars rebuilding a country after destroying their infrastructure." The MSS veteran holds up the currency plates.

"When you can buy your enemy's country and just walk in and take it over?"

"What an ingenious plan, White Dragon! You have redeemed yourself in the eyes of the grateful peoples of the Eastern Alliance, comrade."

The silent economic war is waged on America on December 11, 2001.

To be continued …

Contact:tblancey44@gmail.com

Printed in the United States
by Baker & Taylor Publisher Services